MATING BIRDS

Lewis Nkosi

Ravan Press  Johannesburg

First published in South Africa 1987
by Ravan Press (Pty) Ltd.
P.O. Box 31134
Braamfontein 2017
South Africa

Copyright © 1987 by Lewis Nkosi
Cover illustration Melanie Marder Parks

ISBN 0 86975 317 7
Printed by Galvin and Sales, Cape Town

For my grandmother, Esther Makatini,
who washed white people's clothes
so that I could learn to write

MATING BIRDS

In a few days I am to die. Strange, the idea neither shocks nor frightens me. What I feel most frequently now is a kind of numbness, a total lack of involvement in my own fate, as though I were an observer watching the last days in the life of another man.

Every morning I stand at this small grilled window, gazing at the sky, which is a marvelous blue at this time of year; the air is as clear, as hard as frost, and the sunlight has a soft shimmering quality to it: it blinds the eye; it dazzles. Sometimes a flock of birds will ascend the sky, wings beating wildly; often a pair will mate up there in freedom and open space, clinging to each other joyfully in the bright air as though for dear life. Then, no longer able to restrain himself, the male will attempt to inject his sperm into the female and he, of course, as often as not, will miss so that you can see his pale seed dripping through the air while the female giggles wildly, as is the habit of her sex.

The scenario is the same every morning. The mating birds caw, they whir and whirl outside my window and the smell of fresh spring sharpens the air with its lush, acrid promise. All the same, it is mostly the birds pairing in the open sky that remind me with a vivid poignancy I rarely feel these days why I'm locked up in this tiny cell, awaiting death by execution. I move my hand toward the window and the sunlight, and try to imagine the colors of the Indian Ocean in the early morning light when the water is already flecked with brilliant sunspots or in the early afternoon when, hardly moving at all, the water turns into shiny turquoise.

I can see it all quite clearly: the beach, the children's playgrounds, the seafront hotels, and the sweating, pink-faced tourists from upcountry; the best time of all is that silent, torpid hour of noon when the beach suddenly becomes deserted and, driven back to the seafront restaurants and the temporary shelter of their hotel rooms, crowds of sea bathers suddenly vanish, leaving behind them not only the half-demolished cheese and tomato sandwiches but sometimes an occasional wristwatch, an expensive ring, or a finely embroidered handkerchief still smudged with lipstick from a pair of anonymous lips. Not infrequently, the tourists leave behind them an even worthier trophy—a young body lying spent and motionless on the warm white sands to be gazed at by us, the silent forbidden crowds of non-white boys in a black, mutinous rage.

That, after all, is how I first saw the English girl one afternoon, lying on an empty stretch of Durban beach as though washed up by the tide after an all-night storm: she was a golden statue, lovely and broken among the ruins of an ancient city, and yet for all that, she was shockingly alive, dripping suntan oil and glowing with the sun that beat upon her elongated body. Her flesh was surrendered, as it were, to the hungry gaze of African youths who combed the beach every day for lost or discarded articles.

2

Oh, I have often wondered (as most men are apt to wonder, when it is too late and the game is already lost) how my life would have turned out had I not gone to the beach that hot October day, or, having gone to the beach, if I had stayed well within the limits of my side of the beach instead of poaching so close to what is known as the "Whites Only" bathing area. Would I be languishing in this prison cell now, awaiting death by hanging, or would I have lived to fulfill my ambition of becoming the first truly great African writer my country has ever produced—a future that so many of my friends and teachers had so confidently predicted for me? Frankly, I don't know. In any case, it is too late now to speculate on such matters. On Friday, as surely as the sun rises from the east, they will hang me. They will take me out of my cell; they'll ask me to mount the last steps to the scaffold; and on the appointed hour, dazed, drugged, and blindfolded, I will step into a void and the knives will swish. I will have time to remember only the judge's dire sentence: "For the despicable crime you have committed, I command that you should be taken to a place of execution, there to be hanged by the neck until you are dead, and may God have mercy on your soul!"

Hard words! Bloodcurdling words! Yet I hold no grudge against the judge. As he himself was at pains to point out during the trial, he was merely carrying out his duties; his own personal feelings did not enter into the matter at all. And to be quite honest, am I myself so sure that I am entirely blameless of the crime I am supposed to have committed? Everything happened so quickly in that seaside bungalow that I could hardly reflect at the time how much of what happened was wholly of the girl's bidding, how much the result of my own wayward impulse. What I have come to understand very clearly is how the seeds of my own destruction were planted the very first day I laid eyes on the girl lying on the sands of the Durban beach, for what happened later was surely the final ripening of those seeds and the harvesting of the grain of lustful ambition that had grown in a matter of weeks until it had matured like a powerful weed to consume my life.

It is too late now to reflect on my father's warning, so

often repeated to all young men bound for the city. Had the old man not often warned: "Never lust after a white woman, my child. With her painted lips and soft, shining skin, a white woman is a bait put there to destroy our men. Our ways are not the ways of white people, their speech is not ours. White people are as smooth as eels, but they devour us like sharks." And so it had proved. Needless to say, at the time I had not paid any attention to the cranky old man and his warnings. Not until I had swallowed the bait and the hook was already twisting in the gullet did I remember my father's words. That day on the beach, when I came across the English girl, I saw only what White Authority, with the aid of so many laws and legal penalties, had forbidden me to see. Another human being. A woman with a body that was soft and round and desirable. And within reach. That is what I saw.

Separated only by a small stream from the non-white section of the beach, the girl was lying flat on her stomach, her brown head sheltered in the crook of her arms. I stopped in my path. It wasn't simply that her skimpy bikini covered very little of her generous curves; she seemed never to have bothered to conceal anything. In fact, her bra was unclasped from the back. She had then eased it down from her smooth shoulders so that once or twice when she shifted her body on the towel I was able to glimpse a pale wink of flesh from under her compressed bosom.

I remember something else too: behind the girl's inert body was the inevitable notice board bearing the legendary warning: BATHING AREA—FOR WHITES ONLY! A sign that immediately filled me with rage. Had the girl needed protection against the blazing October sun, the shadow that the billboard cast over the sand would have certainly provided it; but she did not seem to need it. She lay there, heavy, slack, motionless, roasting in the sun, the damp hair clinging to the nape of her neck. There was no breeze, no air, no sound anywhere except the muffled splash of the water lapping gently against the dark rocks of the beach. Exposed, isolated, she was alone there—or so it seemed—inhabiting a marginal world between the despised, segregated blacks and the indifferent, privileged whites who looked upon us Africans as interlopers on a beach that many felt should have been completely set aside for them. For ten minutes I watched her, mesmerized, not daring to make my presence known to her, and in all that time she had hardly moved. To this day I do not know what took hold of me then, but suddenly as I gazed at her prostrate form I felt a feverish, almost uncontrollable desire for the girl. Though now I have had sufficient time to review the events that led to the encounter, I am certain what I felt for her was not exactly sexual desire for a body I must have known I could never possess, the race laws being what they are in South Africa; no, it was something more, something vaster, sadder, more profound than simple desire. Mingled with that feeling was another emotion: anger.

Yes, it was anger I felt for that girl. A sudden, all-consuming fury and blinding rage. She lay there in my path like a jibe, a monstrous provocation, and yet she was not really aware of my presence. People like her never are. Her eyes closed, her mouth slightly open as though ground to dust by a nameless, tameless lust, she was asleep, mindless of the suffering she caused, just as she was mindless of the sun and the breeze that riffled through her rich brown hair as through the wealthy pages of a smutty book.

It was while I was looking at the fine pores of her skin, at the red roots of her brown hair, that the girl opened her eyes. They were funny eyes, wide and green and shot with violet like a glowing winter fire. She seemed not at all surprised to see me there. Perhaps it was part of the provocation, but for a whole minute she stared into my eyes, neither smiling nor scowling, simply and openly staring, giving an impression of a person taking off her clothes in the presence of a lover from whom there was no need to conceal anything. There was in her expression the offer of a familiarity for which nothing had prepared me, a familiarity with which I therefore felt unable to deal with any confidence: her scrutiny lacked either coquetry or artifice and therefore did not accord with her being there at all. If, for instance, she had shown some hesitation, or if she had batted her eyelids or fumbled quickly with her towel or bikini, I might have known what she was after. Her smile, her striptease act, her calculated coyness, would have betrayed an interest, an awareness, but she did none of these things; neither did she smile.

I suppose I should have looked away then. Perhaps it was what she expected: to browbeat me into losing face. At any rate, I should have acted as all "good natives" do in the presence of a white woman, above all one who is without any clothes on. I should have kept my eyes, as they say, where they belong. But I did not; I did not act like a black who knew his place. I doubt if this was a simple case of boldness or defiance. I was compelled by something in the girl's eyes that was ludicrously simple, open, naked, and undemanding, a sort of acknowledgment of myself as a person inhabiting the same planet as herself.

I cannot exactly describe the emotion I felt at that moment when, the challenge having been given and accepted, our eyes stayed locked in a sickening and unloving embrace like exhausted swimmers trying to stay above water, still sinking but holding fast to each other if only to stay alive. It was then that imperceptibly the girl shifted her position on the towel, bringing her right arm across her bosom to cover up her breasts while with the left she cleverly maneuvered to hook up her bra behind her back. This action, done with a certain amount of boredom and calculated negligence, offered a fleeting glimpse of a pale breast with its nipple puckered into a pointed tip of frilled purple flesh. For the first time, sick, ashamed, and aroused, I looked away. Looked away but too late to make any difference; for having looked and seen what was not meant for my eyes to see, I became marked forever with the sign of Cain. Already the curse was beginning its work. After a minute, when I was sufficiently calm, I stood up. Got up, staggered. I was slightly dizzy from the glare of the sun. I found that I couldn't see properly and a severe headache was coming on. Rapidly, not wishing to look back immediately, I began to walk away and when I did look back the girl was sitting up, her arms clasped around her knees, her head bent to one side like a child who has been deprived of something dear. She was watching my departure with more than casual interest.

3

So far as my jail treatment goes I have nothing to complain about. Indeed, from the moment the death sentence was passed on me my situation improved considerably. My cell was made more comfortable, the food became noticeably better, I was allowed to have pen and paper and whatever books I desired. Not to put too fine a point on it, it is the very height of irony that, vile as my crime is held to be, I have become in my last days something of a folk hero, a kind of celebrity in a country where celebrities are rare. Were I a popular singer or a cinema star, were I a heart-transplant surgeon or a popular politician, nothing in the form of public adulation that is accorded to such performers could approach, let alone surpass, the kind of public recognition I have begun to attract as a university-educated native who went bad; a native who in order to gain a glimpse of a white paradise, of that heaven from which many blacks are excluded, tore up barriers, trampled down fences, and defied custom and convention to sleep with a lily-white "virgin" woman. That the girl was no better than a high-class tart, really, who earned her living by stripping before white businessmen at some Durban beach nightclub, has been conveniently forgotten by everyone. Instead, my wild temptress has become a saint, a tender white virgin who became the unwitting victim of the most despicable sexual crime. What beefy, red-faced Afrikaner farmers from the *platteland* come down to the coast to see is a "Kaffir Boy" who had the temerity, the audacity to seize a "respectable" white woman in her bungalow and insert his horrible, oversized "black thing" into her—*Here my nadir!* The very thought of it is enough to bring tears to their eyes. They come and peer through the grill as I take my turn at physical exercises, and at their first glimpse of the ravisher I can see first surprise, then doubt, and finally disappointment on their faces. Is this the boy who performed such miracles with a white woman? After all, did not the prosecution speak of scars and bruises left by my hands on the girl's body? Did they not mention ripped-off clothes and fingerprints around each breast? Did they not speak of love bites, of torn lips, and other lacerations on the neck? Did they not allude to the fingermarks on the breasts and shoulders; and finally the signs of superhuman struggle that resulted in furniture being overturned and the bed board collapsing? No, this they cannot believe!

My white scrutinizers seem to suspect that a subtle joke is being played on them. My size is too small and unimpressive, my member is not hard and permanently erect for everyone to see. I do not possess any horns sprouting obligingly from the sides of my head. Indeed, it would be difficult to find anywhere a more regular fellow, a more banal-looking African. In my prison uniform I remind my white visitors too much of their garden boys and house servants.

Only the ladies will not let go of the notion that I incarnate some dark, devilish force with which it is sufficient merely to come into contact to be marked for life. Dressed in their Sunday-best finery, delicately rouged, gloved and hatted, their faces sometimes veiled against what I can only assume they regard as the presence of a contagious disease, they stand discreetly behind their menfolk, their hands behind their backs, watchful, tense, and ready to ward off an attack. Sometimes the men will spit on the ground and shout imprecations as they leave. "Dirty black bastard! I wish they'd hang you twice over for what you did."

But for all that, I am well treated by my jailers. As I say, I have become something of a celebrity toward whom even the prison-governor feels a certain amount of pride and satisfaction. This may surprise many, but it is easy enough to explain. After all, it is my crime, as well as my presence in this nondescript jail, that has drawn attention to the governor and his staff and has brought observers from international organizations and news correspondents from some of the best papers in the world. Inevitably, some of the limelight reflects on the governor and his staff. Minute details of my behavior, based on round-the-clock observations by trained personnel, are made available to men who are contributing their knowledge and expertise to the growing body of sexual criminology. They come to pay me a visit, often they stay to spend a pleasant afternoon, drawing me out about the kind of life I led as a child. They ask pertinent questions about my parents, my teachers, the sexual practices indulged in by black people. Others, I'm sure, would like to examine my somewhat—well, yes, let us admit it—oversized penis; but usually they are shy and polite, eager to preserve throughout the air of a serious, earnest inquiry into the mental life of a rapist. All the same, the excited curiosity aroused in my observers by the slightest revelation of anything relating to sexual matters borders on the morbid and unsavory. Some of the questions are startlingly naive. A few are searching enough. They all end the same way. What made me do it? Had I always entertained a wish to go to bed with a woman of a superior race? And in retrospect, though admittedly the conditions were not ideal, did I find the lady in question was as sexually capable as a black woman? And, finally, suppose an uprising by the blacks were to take place, would every native go on the rampage, raping every white woman and child in sight? And so it goes on and on and on!

All this is strange, very, very strange. In fact, to say that my situation is somewhat peculiar would be to understate the case. For instance, how can we account for the fact that though I am a rapist, convicted before the courts for defiling the sanctity of a white woman's flesh, the treatment I am receiving from my jailers contrasts so curiously with that meted out to political prisoners who have done no more than demand equal rights for all in our country? Though these men have committed no violence, from what I hear and from the evidence daily proffered to the courts, their mode of detention is an outrage to the civilized conscience. Often they are starved, beaten, and tortured to the limits of their endurance. Instead of receiving assistance from the state, their families are harassed, bullied, and to all intents and purposes, punished just as much as if they themselves were guilty of crimes against the state.

My own case, as I said, is different: I suffer no such brutalization. Indeed, were I not a candidate for the hangman's noose, my confinement, such as it is, would be no more than a form of irritation, at worst an inconvenience; or perhaps a welcome if enforced retirement from a world that, to be quite honest, I have always found grubby, mean, uncharitable, a place in which the best in us contends with the worst, with human greed, destructive lust, and vanity of every kind. But for me all that is over. Here in jail, protected by brick walls and barbed wire, I have at last conquered some of the worst appetites of my flesh; instead of weaving fantasies of more and better contrived sexual gratification, I spend my last days in meditation. I hope to preserve these fruits of self-scrutiny for posterity on cheap, unimpressive notepaper with which I have been provided by the authorities in order, as so many have urged me, to write the story of my life.

4

The story of my life? Everyone wishes to know the story of my life! Prison authorities, newspaper editors, students of human psychology, above all, connoisseurs of human oddity, they all come to me with avid expressions on their faces, their ears strained to catch every word I let fall. It is a modern disease, this appetite for facts that, once obtained, it is hoped, will explain everything. Else how to account for the trouble everyone takes, the expenditure in time and money? One man, a European of Swiss-German background, has flown all the way from Zurich (everything in our age apparently leads back to the Trier on the Moselle or to Zurich and Vienna, to the *Interpretation of Dreams* and *The Communist Manifesto*). This man has left everything behind, his job, his family, his wealthy patients, to come and see me, to inquire, to prod, to probe. A large, sober-looking man in flashing, rimless glasses, Dr. Emile Dufré speaks in a slow, courteous manner, using the persistent questioning routine familiar to those who seek to unravel the mysteries of the unconscious as physicians use instruments for sounding and testing for defects in an unhealthy body. Dr. Dufré gives the impression of vast calm, of restfulness. He is patient, he is unhurried. Over and over again he asks the same questions, only rephrasing them to avoid monotony, or worse still, in order to avoid giving the impression of not believing what I tell him. With this man, huge, white, bespectacled, friendly but remote, childhood stories are a speciality. Again and again he asks about my mother; he asks about my feelings toward my father. Did I ever wish to kill him, or perhaps did I not secretly hope that while my father was cutting the trunk of a tree, the tree would come crashing over his head. When I laugh, Dr. Dufré remains imperturbable. "You think it never happens?" he asks. "You will be surprised how often children wish catastrophe to befall their parents!"

"Of course, it happens," I say, unable to stop myself from laughing. "Only why should I wish it to happen? My father and I got along very well."

I am sorry. I have gone to school. I know what the man wants. I have read a great deal that surprises and amuses me. Are these not, after all, the men who believe that feces are to a child what money in the bank is to an adult?

My African visitors are refreshingly different. They ask no questions about my father or my mother, whether or not I come from a broken home or a happy one. These visitors, who must be as curious as anyone else, come and sit in the visitors' room talking of matters far removed from sexual crimes. They talk of the weather, of the drought, and of the ruined countryside after the last year's spring rains have carried the soil off into the ocean. After that they stop and let me talk while they listen. It is a magnificent well-tried method, this silence, never asking any questions. A trap. It opens me up. At such times it is I who *want* to talk; it is I who want to mention everything. At such moments I am like a clock that has been fully wound up and suddenly needs a release. I want to tell everything, to leave out nothing!

"How can I describe how it happened?" Talking of the day the English girl and I slept together, I pause to look at each one in turn. "It was like a dream, like sleepwalking. We met as usual, as though by design, at the usual spot on the beach. As was her custom, she got undressed and lay down to sunbathe. I, too, lay down to sun myself. I was on my 'Black side' of the beach and she was on her 'White side.' When it was time to leave, she got up and walked the same way she had always walked—across the sand dunes, through the clump of woods, while I followed at a discreet distance." And thus I go on, and while I talk, my African visitors do not look at me. Their heads are bent, they stare at my feet as though fascinated by their shapes. All that indicates they are listening, even if they are unconvinced, is the occasional African moan or hum, "Mmh!"

All the same, I feel the urgent need to explain myself:

"The bungalow was in a back street, near the football grounds. It was raised six feet from the ground by wooden supports. A flight of wooden steps led up to the door. The girl seemed tired. She climbed each one of those steps with a heavy, noiseless tread, carrying on one arm her beach towel, on the other her basket. When she had reached the last step, she paused, her hand on the latch, and gazed down at me, a cryptic smile on her face. Then she entered, leaving the door slightly open. And while I gazed at her, surprised, she began to undress right there in front of me . . ."

Even when I fall back exhausted with the urgency of my confessions, my African visitors say nothing. They express no surprise. They sigh and press the fingers of their hands together and say nothing. Above all, they observe. I can see them watching me when they think I am not looking. In this way, simply by watching and by listening, they are at last able to form an opinion of me. They are able to make up their minds as to what kind of person I am. Am I capable, as the court seems to have been convinced I was, of seizing a solitary white woman in a cottage by the sea and ravishing her against her will? My visitors express no opinion; they only listen to what I have to say; later they will make up their minds about me.

These people, the old uncles and the aunts, some of whom are mere links in a long chain that forms the extended family, I have never seen before now—at any rate, these people listen not to the words I speak but to something behind the voice, something that ought to match the expression in my face but may not. To these people, I suddenly realize, my rapid speech, the constant shifts of tone and flights of fancy, the unexpected flashes of wit and irony, create an impression of emotional instability, of discontentedness, which leaves them in doubt as to my moral soundness. I do not speak like them. In my voice, in the quick rhythms of my speech, there is something alien, a wanton disregard for the proprieties of formal discourse in which one Zulu telling a story to another brings to the narrative the constraints of courtly dignity sometimes in a manner so haltingly circumspect as to cause a listener waiting for the point of the story to groan aloud in suppressed torment.

Quite clearly these are qualities I do not possess. A bitter man, secretive and isolated, sometimes I speak too quickly, sometimes too hesitantly, often lapsing into long surly silences. And from this style alone, because of centuries of practice in forming judgment of human character on the basis of human speech, by the time I leave, my visitors seem to have concluded that I am not to be trusted; my ways are no longer their ways. They have come to the view that I am now as foreign to them as the white girl they have been observing in the witness box with whom I am said to have coupled, a woman as pale as a piece of paper, whose hair is long like that of a goat and whose lips are painted the color of red ocher.

Finally, they leave, my visitors. As they troop out into the noise and sunshine of the prison yard, their eyes avoiding mine, the message is as clear as if they had spoken. I am not to be trusted. Even if I am to die for them I no longer exist. In reality I have become a stranger, a shadow with whom they have nothing in common. So once again I am alone, but it was not always thus. In essence, this is what I tell the man from Zurich, my constant visitor, my interrogator, my confessor.

5

Every day I talk to Dr. Dufré, the eminent Swiss criminologist, who is compiling a dossier of my case "for the augmentation of scientific knowledge," as he quaintly puts it. When I am not talking to the great Swiss doctor of mental health, I am engaged in writing my life story. It helps to pass the time.

A great discipline, writing. One might even say it is character-forming were the observation not likely to sound a trifle odd in the mouth of one already condemned to hang for the crime of raping a white woman. All the same, I derive great satisfaction from writing. I write all the time. The thought of death, the horror of departing from this world before my time is served, so to speak, puts new zeal into my pen.

I sit at a small wooden table by the grilled window of my cell. The table is heaped with cheap prison paper, and with the enthusiasm of a man partaking of the last meal before setting out on a long and arduous journey, I write the story of my life. I write of my first encounter with the English girl, of my subsequent arrest, of my trial and conviction. I write not in an orderly fashion, not even chronologically, but randomly, setting down what memory thrusts to the forefront of my diseased mind, with a hasty if confined feeling of relief. Relief, if I may say so, not unlike sexual release.

Let me also mention the fact that in writing my story, I have tried not to loose a grip over my emotions. That is very important. A kind of taut moral compactness is what I have aimed for, phrases rounded up and cut down to size like blocks of ice. Self-pity and sentimentality are two faults, I hope, I shall never be accused of by those who will have the opportunity to read what I have set down in these note-papers. I may not have always succeeded, of course, but at least I have tried. I have tried to see everything keenly, nakedly, despite the fact that human motives are always mixed, at the best of times a very complicated affair. Above all, I have tried to explain as much to myself as to the hordes of anonymous readers—my hypocritical brothers and sisters —who will read, judge, and accuse me with how I came to feature in what has become the most celebrated case of "indecent assault and rape" in the annals of South African crime.

You may think, and quite rightly so in my opinion, that the notoriety attached to this case has come about not so much from the repugnant nature of the crime itself as from its racial undertones. In short, the girl is white and I am black. I cannot possibly disagree with such a just and generous interpretation of the facts, for everyone knows that I am to hang not simply for raping *a girl* but for having slept with a *white* woman; for having aspired, so to speak, to what South African whites imagine is the height of sexual bliss. Still, let us not labor the point.

I have said as much to Dr. Dufré, this funny man who comes to hear what I have to say, who scans my face, who interrogates, who scribbles and compares the notes with what I have written. As a Jew who has seen much that is odd and unpleasant in the world, Dufré has the patience and professional curiosity that make him an ideal listener. To begin with, I try to describe to him the impulse that drew me to the English girl in a country where even to look at a white woman is to court daylight beatings and worse. I cannot yet make clear even to myself what came over me that hot sultry November day when, walking behind the English girl who wore her usual red-and-yellow-flowered wrap, I followed her up the dunes into the secluded beach-side cottage and watched her while she unwrapped herself like a gift and lay naked, fully stretched out on the bed with the door wide open. I trace the sequence of events from the very first day that I clapped my eyes on the girl lying spent and motionless on a lonely stretch of Durban beach, the days and weeks afterward when I watched her slim figure slack, pink, and hot with sun, stretched on the sands of the beach like an elongated fish washed up by the tide after an all-night storm, to the moment when during a hasty coupling, spurned and overwrought with desire, I struggled with the girl's naked body while she screamed and cursed until the police and neighbors came running through the open door. Like a madman, I remember that even after I had heard the noise of approaching footsteps and the sound of excited voices getting closer all the time, and with half the furniture overturned—the prosecution later made much of this fact—and the girl screaming and kicking, I remember that my one thought was to return, by force if necessary, to that narrow fount, to the source of all forbidden pleasure where I had just been welcomed and then ejected. To this day, my eyes shut, I can still see her white naked body; I can still remember the smell of sun-drenched hair and the salty taste of fine sweat and seawater where I pressed my mouth on her breast.

When Dufré is gone, I write down what I have been relating to him while it is still fresh in my mind. I write it down rapidly in longhand, with a steady and sober accumulation of details, coaxing the memory, which at best is unreliable, or at the very worst treacherous. For pen and paper (for what is by any South African standards an extreme indulgence) I have to thank the intervention of the Minister of Justice, who was satisfied that my request for books and writing paper could not in itself constitute a threat to public security and good order. What possible behavior by an African prisoner who is convicted of the sexual crime of rape could constitute the so-called threat to public security and good order, the prison authorities never cared to explain. No matter. This may have been simply one of those official phrases of which the South African government is an acknowledged master. When I finish writing, I push the stacked up pages aside. I get up from my table and walk up to the small grilled window of the tiny cell I occupy alone —another form of indulgence—where I gaze at the empty sky for minutes on end, like someone waiting for rain to fall.

6

Throughout the proceedings and within the strict meaning of the game they were asked to play, the judges of the Supreme Court have been scrupulously fair to me. My rights have been mentioned, the police have been urged repeatedly to do nothing to abrogate them. The fact that the girl I'm supposed to have ravished is white became, no doubt, the source of recurring embarrassment for everyone connected with the case, for that fact alone meant that everyone had to live with the nagging suspicion that the real point of this trial was not the rape of a girl but the color of the alleged rapist as much as that of the victim. But how can this fact be acknowledged without doing incalculable harm to the cause of justice upon which the very existence of the judges depends, to say nothing of their supposed impartiality and incorruptibility, a matter that involved their highest personal dignity! So everyone except my lawyer talks around what is the main issue, which, though unspoken, remains at the very center of the trial, a festering sore contaminating the air with its odor of racial conspiracy.

The moment I was shoved into the dock and, blinking into the light of day, saw the judges sitting on the dais in their scarlet robes and white wigs, solemn, rosy-cheeked, yet grim and determined, I said to myself, they are going to hang me. Even before they had heard my side of the story I knew they were going to hang me. Something about the way they avoided looking into my eyes or the exasperating display of expansive courtesy with which they favored me at the slightest provocation alerted me to the fact that they were going to hang me. I said to myself, *I'm fair game for them! They are after my neck!* But they were in no hurry to press their claims. All the same, if I needed any proof of the Chief Justice's intention, the pitiless smile, wan and carefully put on like his cravat, convinced me long before he pronounced sentence that in his own mind he had already found me guilty.

I know it may seem ungrateful and even petulant of me to say it, but in a long and dreary trial of this kind the judge's kindness is the most intolerable feature of the proceedings: the beaming smile shines down from on high into the well of the court like the bright flash of an avenging sword. And when His Lordship periodically asks the court orderly, with the concern of a high-minded executioner anxious for the welfare of his victim, whether or not my cell conditions are satisfactory, or when in a quavering, highly strung voice he demands to know whether anything can be done to improve my diet and the comfort of my bedding, I know what to expect. Even more disturbing is the judge's interest in my capacity to concentrate on the proceedings. Leaning forward a bit in his chair, his iron-gray head tilted slightly to the side as if to listen to some extraterrestrial voice, Chief Justice Milne addresses the prosecution in a tone full of heavy public concern for the rights of a citizen: "In view of the Accused's tendency to fall asleep in the middle of an important piece of testimony," he observes "can this court be assured that everything is being done to enable him to get a good night's sleep?"

The query causes consternation as much among the police officers as among the white citizens in the public galleries. Such solicitude for the comforts of a black man is frankly unheard of in our country. But I am no fool. I know then with an absolute certainty that this Judge is out to hang me. If I had not suspected it before, his repeated expressions of concern for my safety and comfort convince me he is out to hang me. I have had sufficient opportunity to study the form of these proceedings. I have heard many judges who only minutes before cheerfully exchanged anecdotes with a prisoner in the dock, judges who tirelessly harassed and obstructed a prosecutor during the conduct of the trial. I have seen them suddenly lower their heads as though in prayer and in a tone of eerie vibrant emotion, sometimes accompanied by a farcical jerking of the face into tearful compassion, I have heard them suddenly declare, "I find the

Accused guilty of all the charges under the law. Have you anything to say in mitigation before I pass sentence?'' Such an abrupt change in the judge's manner is always astounding, not to say shocking. A prisoner who has unwittingly put too much trust in the judge's apparent compassion during the proceedings or even the frank expressions of affection is thus always caught unawares by such a complete turnabout. Startled and puzzled by this unexpected turn in their fortunes, I have seen hardened criminals turn gray with shock before fainting in the dock. That is not how I wish to make my exit from this world.

7

Sitting in the gloomy courtroom, it was sometimes difficult to avoid the impression that some elaborate primitive game was daily being played by the minions of the Justice Department with no other objective in mind save the fulfillment of some deeply atavistic need for ritual. There was the Chief Justice himself, for example, and his two assessors, whom he addressed solemnly as "My Brother Judges," in their scarlet robes, their heads bewigged like those of some African medicine men presiding over some dark ceremonial proceedings. Their heads would bob up and down. They would nod gravely. But when they held themselves completely still, which could last for a whole intolerable minute while they listened to a piece of long evidence, their solemn impassive faces presented a profound metaphor for Death.

Kakmekaar, the prosecutor, plays his part with just enough gusto to attract the next day's headlines. But occasionally he is chillingly believable. When he demands that the judges find me guilty as charged, his manner becomes harsh, bitter, personally aggrieved. "The fact, Your Lordships," he reminds the judges, his large-jowled pulpy face growing livid with fury, "that the Accused has a smattering of an education and that shortly before his arrest he had, in fact, been a full-time student at the University of Natal, a privilege that he was soon to abuse by leading illegal demonstrations against university authorities, is one important reason, we feel, that Your Lordships should make an example of him as a deterrent for other misguided natives." Here Kakmekaar pauses to cast a glance at the dock where I sit, flanked by two armed police constables. "I may also add, Your Lordships," he says persuasively, "that the fact that two photographs in gilded frames duly appeared in the Bantu newspaper, which, as I understand, has a considerable circulation among natives without much sophistication, natives who, I venture to suggest, may look up to the accused as a hero who dared to defy the laws of this country, makes it the more urgent, I submit, that should the court find the Accused guilty he should be made to pay the supreme penalty that for crimes of this nature our courts are required to exact. Your Lordships, in a case of this sort I submit that nothing short of capital punishment can suffice.

Until such time as white women of this city, I dare say until such time as white women of this *country,* can walk about freely in the streets and beaches of our towns without fear of molestation, our police and our courts are obliged to see to it that everything is done to uphold the law. Until that time, Your Lordships, our womenfolk—our mothers and sweethearts and our sisters—will find it increasingly difficult to venture out-of-doors without fully armed escorts!''

For a moment, deeply moved by his own eloquence, the prosecutor collapses into a chair and mops his brow with a suitably large and very white handkerchief, visible to even those sitting way back in the public galleries. But the judges, I am glad to say, look pained and embarrassed by the eagerness with which the prosecutor presses his claims. After all, though they are white, the justices are devoutly wedded to the formal demands, if not the spirit, of justice. The game, if game this is, must be played strictly according to the rules. So the judges peer with anxious imploring eyes toward my defense counsel, a small, dapper, darkly handsome figure, with a covert invitation that he, too, should play his part in the game in order to endow the proceedings with the necessary legitimacy.

From the dock I watch everything. No gestures escape me. Watching them play their roles, the prosecutor, the judges, the scandalized members of the public, is my way of dealing with the ennui that spreads like an epidemic around me. I also watch the girl, Veronica Slater, who, after giving her evidence, sits in the front row of the white galleries, intolerably beautiful in her knitted ensemble of white dress and white coat, with a sloppy, wide-brimmed hat to match. Today she looks different. In the intensity of the sun of the beach I remember only too well the girl who, not pale, not angelic and ethereal like this one, but warm, pink, and lush, turned swiftly on the towel, the hotness of the sun gathered into the pinkness of her sunburned tan. In court, surrounded by her own kind, Veronica looks extremely white and vulnerable, like an unreal thing evoked out of the gloom with the trick of some magical sleight of hand. She looks the very symbol of purity and light, of saintly flesh, raped, violated by the brutal force of a dark continent. It is as if I am seeing her for the first time. From a window above her a light shines into the courtroom, but it does not entirely relieve the gloom in which she sits, her long beautiful legs pressed together, her hands clasped and resting calmly on her lap. Rather, it shines straight across the room, toward the dock in which I sit, enfolded in the castle of my skin. It is against this light, trying to see Veronica's face, that I sometimes lose its distinctness. All I can see is the blur of whiteness that blinds by its very glare.

My counsel, Max Siegfried Müller, Q.C., is the most celebrated advocate for the oppressed and the downtrodden in our country. An old man with a white lion-mane on his back, a vast forehead and square jaw, a pair of penetrating blue eyes, he is, of all surprising things, considering where he is now, a refugee from Nazi Germany who came to South Africa at the young age of twenty-four. He is known as the scourge of the Establishment, of the ill-trained and inexperienced magistrates and prosecutors. Small and dapper, always elegantly got up in Saville Row pinstriped suits, he conducts himself with a deliberate calmness, calculated to present the most striking contrast to the exultant, most extravagant histrionics of the prosecution. When he rises, he speaks softly, with a courteous disdain for the depth of his opponent's legal argument. With mock desperation, he addresses himself to the grateful judges: "Your Lordships, I must urge My Illustrious and Learned Friend, Meneer Kakmekaar, I must try and curb his instinct for blood. I know this may be asking him to place upon himself an intolerable and perhaps impossible restraint, but really he must try! Not a day passes in this court without My Learned Friend being heard to importune Your Lordships for a speedy dispatch of my client to the gallows. I have to remind My Learned Friend this is a court of justice, not a butcher's shop!"

This kind of thing goes on for days on end. The heat in the courtroom is unbearable. Outside, the sun shines from a naked and indifferent sky. But inside the courtroom the indifference is cloaked with the significance of symbolic action. I am the eternal goat being prepared for sacrificial slaughter; and, of course, I'm bored with the prolonged but clearly necessary preparations for the ceremonial shedding of blood.

When I am not in court, listening to the gradual accumulation of the evidence against me, evidence pieced together from the testimony of witnesses who apparently enjoy nothing better than giving vivid descriptions of sexual details in cases of this kind—government pathologists who, though careful to show their distaste and discomfort, gleefully mention the results of painstaking laboratory tests of drops of semen found in the girl's body or those among the chief medical examiners, who with the greatest devotion to duty, tell the court how they stripped the girl and raked her body for clues of physical struggle and violation

—when these men have favored the court with the minutest detail of what they found—love bites on the girl's neck and shoulder and left breast; when the police officers speak angrily but eagerly, without much prompting, of torn pieces of underwear, of furniture overturned, of blood and fingerprints and the stains of sexual intercourse left on the bedclothes and the carpet; when the gruesome details have been mentioned and pored over by the judges and the court rises regretfully at the end of each session, clearly with hopes for even more lurid details to come, a black sedan car arrives to take me away under armed guard as befits a celebrity that I have become! With a slow, monarchal progress I am then driven through the busy city streets, back to my prison cell, where I sit for hours under a dim light, reading, writing, and reflecting on the human condition.

Every day, the sedan invariably took the same route, which surprised me for what it revealed of the appalling laxity in security arrangements. From the Supreme Court, a large Victorian building, old and gray with the accumulation of bird droppings, we would drive down through the gardens, with only one stop at the traffic lights. Nothing is better than the view of the Indian Ocean from the brow of this hill, but the court building itself is a disappointment. In a city famous for its evergreen trees, for flowers forever blooming in and out of season, the Court stands stark and austere on dusty ground bereft of anything green. On the perimeter of the court grounds, a parking lot, a girls' school, and a building that serves as chambers for counsel are all that distinguish a square famous as a seat where a peculiarly South African brand of justice is dispensed. From here the road leads down to the sea, through the racecourse and the city's main shopping area. On a clear day you can see the ocean and the palm-fringed esplanade. It is a calm sea, reflecting nothing of the city's turbulence, nothing of its minor fractious wars, nothing of race riots and economic conflict. From this point you can see the docks and beyond them the stretch of white sands of the Durban beach, shiny like pearls in the day's blazing sun. It was there, six months ago to this day, that I first came across the English girl, Veronica Slater, white, limp, drowsily sunbathing in a no-man's-land between the "Whites Only" section and the rock-strewn "Non-Whites" bathing area. After my expulsion from the university for rebellious conduct, for insubordination and "gross indiscipline," I had taken to loitering on this beach, watching the big liners steaming out of the bay for distant shores of Europe, America, and the Far East. In my mood of profound despondency I was thinking, planning, and dreaming of escape from South Africa, from the life of oppression and wretched exploitation. The girl, too, who appeared so unexpectedly on this strand of beach was perhaps part of this dream of escape. Life plays us so many jokes.

δ

"Shall we start at the beginning, Mr. Sibiya?" is how Dufré
commences one of his many sessions of inquiry into what
he is pleased to term my "possible aberration." Dufré,
my persistent suitor, my solemn inquisitor, the wrecker of
my peace, my torturer. How I hate to see his face sometimes, the pinched, ravenous expression of the eyes, the
hooked nose upon which perch the glinting, rimless glasses.
The very sound of his slightly hoarse voice is a jarring
assault on my ears. Slow and heavily accented but always
meticulous and carefully phrased, Dufré's English retains

the flawless accuracy of a diligently acquired language. His phrasing is measured but pleasureless. It is efficient but devoid of human poetry; acquired, no doubt, after much painful effort and mental application, this linguistic skill, such as it is, shows (in its lack of rhythmic suppleness, its poverty of verbal wit) the many hours of grinding toil that made possible its attainment. But for all its admirable precision, Dr. Dufré's English is also the language of the scientist. It is without a doubt the language of police inquisition and of torture. It has none of the felicity of verbal play, none of the sexual brevity of human speech.

"May I remind you, Mr. Sibiya," he begins, "of your solemnly entered promise to discourse to us on the years of your pastoral childhood, a subject, if I may say so, that is of great clinical interest to my profession."

"Pastoral childhood?" Affecting surprise.

"Yes. I would like to hear of it. It could help us to trace the origins of the obsession, your aspirations to obtain sexual gratification from a female source other than a woman of your own race."

"Why not put it down to a passing whim, Doctor? No more than a passing whim. After all, is it not possible—a momentary loss of control, a madness, frustration . . ." The distinguished doctor looks suitably anguished. These evasions, I know, irritate him, but for me they constitute the only defense I have against the officially sanctioned pryings of bureaucrats and foreign visitors.

In the ghostly twilight of my death cell, with black spiders above us weaving magic webs of finely spun silk in which to capture their unwary victims, the doctor of mental illness and I sit facing each other, not far apart, somber, intimate, as befits the nature of our conversations; nevertheless between us there remains a barrier that neither party wishes easily to acknowledge. The reason is simple enough: a man already condemned to die cannot feel at ease in the presence of another whose life is yet unclouded by the possibilities of imminent death, whose only passion is the excavation of charred seams of the unconscious. Perhaps it is this awareness of what truly separates us that adds to the mid-morning gloom of my death cell. For what in the end can we say to each other, this white man and I, that can break the shell of history and liberate us from the time capsule in which we are both enclosed? What can a Swiss-German Jew say to a black South African convict that can ease the pain and loss and create between us a bridge of communication across vast differences of social background and history? No wonder our conversation, interrupted only by the stray buzzing of a fly or by the sharp echo of a warden's booted footsteps, while it is friendly enough, is also subtly strained, frequently marked by long silences during which the Swiss empties his pipe, fills it very slowly with tobacco from a brown leather pouch he keeps close to his elbow. I can tell from the regular intake and release of breath the immense control the good doctor requires to suppress his internal agitation. All the same, there is nothing faked about my visitor's curiosity, which is truly elephantine. Nothing exhausts his passion for information. "Tell me about your birthplace," he urges.

At this request, I sit up more alertly in the chair. "About Mzimba? There is nothing much to tell about Mzimba, Dr. Dufré."

Dufré smiles solicitously. "Nothing?"

"I mean, it's a country place much like another. There is ample space, the air is pure . . .!" I want to add, "There is even freedom of a kind," but the words do not come naturally to the tongue. The phrase would not fit the emotion I wish to describe. Mzimba? How difficult it is, after years of living in the city, to imagine that puce-colored landscape of steep hills and deep valleys dotted by the thatched Zulu mud huts. On a clear day you could see the white plumes of smoke rising for miles around in a shimmer of brilliant sunshine from the brown clusters of village huts, the broken furrows of red earth marking the dongas where the rain had bitten deeply into the earth. The entire landscape is dominated by the Tugela River, which for seventy miles flows down the narrow, wooded gorges, past vast undulating hills, past the rolling plains upon which herds of Zulu cattle graze solemnly while gazing into the limitless blue of the horizon. From about here, harsh, swift, and unnavigable, the river runs its turbulent course until it reaches the flat coastal plains, where it slows down as it enters the sea.

I was born here and I grew up here, the favorite son of a large Zulu household, loved, cherished, and made much of by my various "mothers" and various "fathers," by my sisters and brothers, by the many cousins and aunts who normally inhabit a large Zulu kraal. To this day I can remember clearly the vast homestead nestled on the side of a hill, the huts set around the cattle kraal, which is the natural forum of a large Zulu family. A short walk up the incline of this hill and we could look down on one of the most beautiful stretches of countryside in all of Zululand. From the edge of the plateau, visible from about a hundred miles inland, the sea looks perfectly calm. Seen from such a height it seems to be reposing in its watery bed like a slothful woman, bare to the sun and naked to the caressing breeze, with an occasional steamer ploughing its course across the immense blue lagoon. But how capricious and untrustworthy that fine weather! During the day a thick vapor will sometimes get up from the ocean, a strong afternoon breeze will waft the moist vapors inland and, forced to rise by the escarpment, the air will quickly condense before falling down as a rainstorm. Always too sudden, the rainstorms catch everyone unawares. In the morning an angry sun may be blazing from a sky quite cloudless and empty of rain, a sky held in torment like a clay pot above a scorching fire; in the afternoon, smelling damp from the ocean, the *intsingizi* will sob its mystery. Then dark clouds will pile up at the top of the Mzimba mountain, and raindrops as large as the breasts of a young Zulu virgin will roll down from the sky. A man might have crossed the Tugela in the morning; in the evening he is unable to return home, for the river is swollen and turbulent, carrying before it uprooted trees, drowned animals, and, occasionally, even the dead body of some unlucky individual.

These are my memories of Mzimba, of Zululand.

When I was growing up, life at Mzimba was slow and easygoing. As children, we were protected from the knowledge of the larger cruelties that were visited upon black people in the rest of the country. The land was fertile, we had cattle, we grew enough to eat and to spare. As for our white rulers, I did not see my first white man—or, shall I say, my first white woman—until I was fourteen years old, a boy looking much older than his age but as yet to undergo the *thomba* initiation ceremony. The European settlement at Mzimba was about forty miles away, and white people rarely came to our part of the world unless obliged to do so by the nature of their special duties and responsibilities.

Very often I am asked—and who asks this question oftener than my friend, the great Dr. Dufré—how my parents got along together. My answer is simple enough. They got on well. They got on fine. Indeed, if I can venture to put a name to so obscure an emotion as that which binds a woman to a man, I would say my father and my mother *loved* each other, though as a good man and a good Zulu my father would have been embarrassed by a declaration of such a sentiment. Love, who knows what love is? A dog loves his master. A man takes care of his women and his children. Then he is happy. But love? Such talk smacks too much of the kind of weak sentimentality so beloved by our European masters. Still, looking back on their relationship, on their devotion and their fidelity, I have to say, yes, I think my father loved my mother, and perhaps my mother loved my father, too. Certainly, on both sides there was affection, there was physical desire, there was respect.

An old man when he took my mother, Nonkanyezi, to wife, by the time I was born, my father was already married to four other wives by whom he had already sired many sons and daughters, some of whom were themselves already married, with children of their own. As is the usual case in a polygamous household, being the youngest, my mother was also the favorite. A young wife, it seems, has certain advantages over the senior wives. Still vigorous and full of sap where the other wives have become slack and thick-fleshed, not to say a little weary with the burdens of child-bearing, the youngest wife comes bearing youth and a new life to a man already old enough to be her father. She is a tonic. She eases his path to the grave with the gaiety and vitality of a young girl. She may even restore a measure of sexual potency to one already given up on such earthly adventures. Such was the case with my mother.

Only a slip of a girl when she married—I can remember that even when I was already a grown-up boy—my mother was still young, unusually slim and willowy for a Zulu woman, with high pointed breasts, very dark glossy hair, and flashing white teeth. There were many rumors about her. One was to the effect that before she married my father she had been betrothed to a popular praise-singer in the village who at the last moment defaulted on the payment of the bride-money. The scandal had been great; the young man had lost face, but what was loss to the young cub was gain to the Sibiya lion. Much later I had cause to reflect that my mother must have been greatly in love with the gifted young poet, so hushed was her voice when she happened to mention his name, so haunted was the expression in her eyes that long-forgotten shadows seemed to have crawled out of her past to mock her present tranquil existence. Those moments were few and far between, for the rest of the time the only sign my mother gave that much unhappiness had been companion to her girlhood was the frequently noted tendency she had to a high nervous laugh, which occasionally turned her uncheckable mirth into dry hysteria.

Unhappiness is not an emotion that a large Zulu family can allow to dominate one of its members. After a decent passage of time it must be checked, life must go on. After all, that is what a large family is there for. So it was with my mother. Once she had consented to marry my father, her past sorrows were all forgotten. She now seemed content with the way things had turned out. She was the favorite wife of a powerful man, a headman. She was recognized by everyone as a great beauty. Sometimes the subject of her good looks was occasion for mild censure, one might even say fear, among the women of the household. With a mixture of pained admiration and cautious disapproval, older women referred to Nonkanyezi's bright personality, her gaiety, her great spirits. They noted her walk, which was not so much a way of getting there as a brazen invitation to the eyes of men to gaze at what was not properly theirs to admire—the male eyes, as old women were obliged to add, which were already too restless to require any further stimulation. Whenever the youngest wife had occasion to put on her new beads, her bangles, and her flashing anklets, everyone, it seemed, was obliged to hold their breath. Old women protested, old women chided; was not a certain unobtrusiveness in a married woman's behavior more appropriate than this perpetual effort to shine with the brilliant splendor of the rising sun! The old women moaned and shook their heads. After all, who did not know how Nonkanyezi—whose name meant "star"—had been courted by so many young men that in the struggle for the possession of her hand there had been numerous stick fights until that aging wily lion, Sibiya, snatched the prize fawn from the contending cubs?

If my mother knew what people said about her behind her back she gave no indication of it. Life in our village was simple. Life went on. One season followed another.

Though we all lived together as one family, each wife had her own hut where she was her own mistress. The other wives, whom I also called my "mothers," took turns to cook for my father. They also took turns to share his mat. At the time, I was too young, of course, to understand the complicated structure of reciprocal duties and carefully balanced relationships of a Zulu household. During the day, while carrying on their household duties, shelling mealies off the cob or crushing the shelled grain on the special grinding stone, the women would be heard gossiping together in the yard like a lot of clucking hens.

Once or twice Dr. Dufré has discreetly mentioned the subject of my religious upbringing. He has pointed out, for example, that the time of death is the moment when our thoughts are supposed to be elevated to higher, more spiritual things. It is the moment, it is said, when we come face to face with our destiny; the gains are calculated, the losses are counted, and fear of perdition, hope for eternal bliss have the effect of concentrating the mind wonderfully. This may be so, but I have to confess that my religious training, such as it was, leaves me considerably unprepared for meeting my creator. Not even the customary Zulu hope of joining the ancestors, supposing that given the nature of my crime they could welcome me to their august company, awakens in me the smallest enthusiasm. The truth of the matter is, I am lost. To be more precise, I'm doubly lost. Unlike my father, I believe in nothing, neither in Christian immortality nor in the ultimate fellowship with the ancestral spirits. I have no faith in the hereafter. When the time comes for my execution, I will don my hood. I will climb the final steps. When the word is given, I will step into the void and the knives will swish. There will be darkness and nothing. This lack of faith is my loss. It is also my strength. My father was different. In everything touching on religious belief and morals he clung stubbornly to custom and tradition. Day after day he drank his endless herbal concoctions. He prayed to the ancestors. In the special area at the back of the main hut, *emsamo,* surrounded by broad-shaft spears, sacrificial strips of meat, and sacred herbs, he prayed to the ancestral spirits, *amathonga,* sprinkling the floor with *intelezi,* burning incense and licking medicine from his fingers after dipping them rapidly in a burning clay container. He prayed endlessly for guidance, for prudence in the government of his household, for wisdom in the conduct of his personal affairs. The result of all that is that I am here about to hang for the rape of a white woman. I can imagine him wherever he is asking himself, "Gods of my Fathers! Where did I go wrong?"

As children, we saw very little of father. It was often said by those who knew about these things that at his time of life the old man found it more congenial to converse with the ancestral spirits whom he was about to join than to hold daily tittle-tattles with members of his own family, whose company he now found only irksome and a source of constant irritation. During his last days with us, the old man had become a mere shadow of whose existence we were all dimly aware, but whose hard substance it became harder and harder to grasp. Occasionally we saw him, solemn-faced and pinched-mouthed, a polished stick in hand, crossing the yard to evacuate himself. At other times, but very rarely now, he was to be seen presiding over the household affairs in the cattle enclosure with the firm but benevolent authoritarianism of a Zulu headman. As far as I can remember, he had become a remote figure, but not unloved for all that.

My mother was different altogether. While the old man represented all that was conservative and unyielding in the Zulu temper, Nonkanyezi was a restless and adventurous spirit, shrewd and energetic, fiercely determined that I should make something of my life far beyond what was expected of a Zulu boy. Toward this end, with infinite patience and cunning, she contrived to send me to school. At first my father opposed the move, but being the favorite wife she found a way around his objections. She spoke glowingly, persuasively, of the opportunities opening up for black people with learning. She conjured up vast empires to be conquered with nothing more powerful than a pen and tutored mind. Respect, a life of ease, and influence were the likely prizes. The old man snorted. Such prospects, as he well knew, were becoming the main lure of the city and the motivating force for the young men to leave their fathers' hearths in search of fame and fortune. What was wrong with tilling the land and raising cattle for beef, and helping to maintain the cohesion of the community that was already severely threatened by outside forces. However, like all traditionalists, my father, I suspect, was also a hard-headed realist, with his eye on the main chance. In a world growing more complex and requiring new, unheard-of skills, sending one son to school was not such a bad idea. To read and write, to communicate messages over long distances, that was part of the magic of the white man everyone wished to acquire.

So my father, whose other children had never learned

to read or write, finally allowed me to be enrolled at the Lutheran Seminary at Mzimba. This also meant, of course, consenting to my conversion and baptism, for the white missionaries extracted a price for imparting knowledge to the children of the pagan race. Before the new pupils could be taught, they had also to embrace the new faith. On this the Church was adamant. Everyone in the village agreed it was a form of blackmail. Equally, everyone agreed, it was a small price to pay for enabling one child in an entire household to acquire knowledge that the white man alone possessed. So this is how temporarily I became an unenthusiastic member of the Zulu Lutheran Church.

9

In the light of my present predicament—I am speaking of my trial and conviction for the very serious crime of raping a white woman, an allegation that, at the risk of repeating myself endlessly, I wish to deny with all the force at my command—there is perhaps one anecdote worthy of mention in connection with my boyhood at Mzimba. It concerns the advice, indeed more than advice, a warning, that my father uttered to me on the eve of my enrollment at the Lutheran Seminary. Oddly enough, this advice preceded a very curious incident with a white family in the white town at Mzimba, which left a deep impression on my young and unformed mind.

The incident was nothing in itself, but the behavior of the white girl, one of the two daughters who accompanied her parents, and the attitude of the Zulu onlookers who witnessed it, soon gave to the incident the quality of an "encounter," an event that was to acquire for me the aura of symbolic meaning. I felt this even more so in the light of the words spoken by my father the day before the trip to Mzimba. "Never lust after a white woman, my child," the old man had pronounced, surveying an old battlefield from the knoll of a hill where the Boer army was once trapped by a Zulu force through the cunning of one of Dingaan's intelligence officers. "With her painted lips and soft, shining skin, a white woman is a bait put there to destroy our men. Our ways are not the ways of white people, their speech is not ours. White people are as smooth as eels, but they devour us like sharks."

I did not say anything to this. I had no idea why my father had chosen to speak in this manner. At the time, it did not occur to me that temptation in the form of a white woman would ever come my way. But my father seemed to be more troubled than I had ever seen him before. "Tomorrow your mother is to take you to the shops at the white town of Mzimba," my father said, not looking directly at me. "This is in preparation for disposing of your body to the white missionaries who will fill your head with all manner of ideas, some of them lies against your own people. I never did hear of anything good that came out of the missionary schools. I have seen the sort of people they bring out, not black, not white, outcasts and misfits who look down on and despise their people. With my own eyes I have seen them in the government offices at Mzimba. Young people who talk to you out of the corner of their mouths while they smoke and blow smoke in your face. They say this is learning. Some, I'm told, even go abroad and marry white women. How can that be? Our ways are not the ways of white people. Their speech is not ours!"

For the first time he turned to me and scrutinized my face. "Your mother says she wants you to drink of the wisdom of the white man. Did your people not have any wisdom of their own before the white men came?" That morning, standing over the crest of the Ophathe Hill and gazing down at the narrow gorge between two hills and beyond at the land where so much blood had already been spilled and, no doubt, more would yet be spilled, a land whose serenity under a clear blue sky seemed to deny that history, I was moved by an obscure emotion that was tinged with fear. In my father's trembling voice, full of apprehension and foreboding, seemed to speak the tongue of an oracle. At Mzimba, the words came back to me, confused and without clear meaning, but thrilling with their damning message. There, amidst the hustle and bustle of excited buyers and sellers, amidst the manic shrieks and squeals of women feverishly helping themselves to household goods that had just been brought in from the big city of Durban, the fresh young maidens and their solicitous suitors snatching greedily at trinkets and all manner of baubles; the noisy crowd constantly streaming in and out of the shop like toothpaste out of a tube; in the middle of this shoving and shouting, having made our purchases from the old Indian merchant, Ahmed Saloojee, of all that I would require for my new career as a pupil of the Lutheran Seminary: the clothes, the lined exercise books, the bright English- and Zulu-language primers, with their gaudy illustrations on every page, which I wasted no time in poring over; having bought all this and many household goods, which was nearly always the object of a trip to Mzimba, and having completed our purchases, my mother and I gathered our goods together and started to walk out of the store through the pressing, sweating crowds. We had hardly reached the top of the veranda when there was a sudden commotion: someone shouting the single word *"Abelungu!"* (white people!) as if a dire warning. Standing on the top steps, I saw for the first time the small comic detachment of a middle-aged white man, his wife and two daughters, all of whom had just alighted from a dilapidated Ford car, climbing up the steps of the store veranda in single file, the man walking slightly in front, his wife and two daughters a fraction behind, the man sweating a little from the effort in his all-too-constricting gabardine suit that was bleached white from overuse and the white straw hat sitting at an angle, his wife looking even hotter and more flushed in her pink-and-white floral dress stained with wet circles under the armpits; but the girls behind them, especially the elder one, looked as cool as cucumbers in their white-and-orange dresses, their hands smooth and delicately gloved, moving easily behind with the grace of young animals. They came up the scuffed wooden staircase in slow, unconfident steps, smiling a little self-consciously at the silent gazing crowd of Zulu onlookers, the girls as cool as the morning in their fresh and crisp linen. When they came to the top of the steps they paused for a moment to allow the crowd to part. My mother was

walking slightly ahead when the crowd began to push back
in deference to the white man. At the same time, it began
to split at two right angles, one section of the crowd sweep-
ing me off with it so that for a second my mother and I were
separated. But very soon, their curiosity still unslaked, the
people behind me started to heave forward like one mighty
river, so that once again I was irresistibly carried forward
on the crest of a new wave, until I found myself right up,
first against the white man, who looked a little surprised at
the stir he and his family were causing. But not entirely
surprised, I guess, since he also knew his power, the power
of all white men. Knew what he could do with it. After all,
as far as he was concerned, we were just a rabble, which he
needed only to lift his arm to cause to part. For a few
seconds, with that instant shock of someone who has seen
a dangerous *mamba* too late to run or extricate himself from
danger, I was able to look very closely into the white man's
eyes before he shooed us off, myself and the pressing crowd
together, like so many frightened birds. I was able to catch
a glimpse not only of the face, the dull sandy hair, the pencil
shade of a growth of beard on his chin, the thin, almost
lipless, mouth. In that fleeting moment I was also able to
register the man's features before I and the rest of the
crowd fell back in a panic.

As I said, I was able to look into the white man's eyes
for one solitary moment of absolute panic. Never had I
seen eyes like that before. Gray and dully impassive, without any light or radiance in them, they seemed to have no
pupils and no center; they were like two flat buttons in a
doll's face. When the white man moved them, they seemed
to change shape again. Now they looked like marbles, he

simply gazed through you with those opaque marbles that resembled the eyes of a blind man. The skin beneath the eyes was sallow and slightly pitted as though the man had suffered appallingly from a skin disease. All these details took only a second or two to observe before I stepped back, as I said, in panic, stumbling as I did so while the man motioned us back, demanding the right of way. He must have spoken then. He must have said something or other, because I saw his lips moving but I did not understand the language. Frightened and now a little desperate with anxiety, I backed away hurriedly, stumbling and falling and getting up again only to find my way blocked by that infernal crowd of pushing, noisy thrill-seekers. The way of escape always came to an end where there was nothing but a solid wall of impassable human flesh. Once again I was being pushed forward, and this time, stumbling forward, I came to rest on my hands and knees like a man genuflecting in prayer in front of the two white girls, who were still coming up behind their mother and father. For a moment, I was down on my knees, sweating and breathing like a steam engine before I scrambled quickly back to my feet in order not to oblige the two girls to have to step over or around me. And now came the first surprise. One of the girls, the elder of the two, who was coming up a few steps behind her mother, paused at the very moment when she was almost on top of me. Glancing around her, she seemed to hesitate while I crouched nervously before her; but there was no sign of anxiety in her own face. She was nonchalantly twirling a bonnet in one hand. Was it a calculated gesture? I cannot tell. Was it a momentary feeling of dread in the middle of a black crowd? I do not know. For an indefinable moment, and those moments can be like an eternity, the girl gazed down at me, her blue eyes pools of wonder and speculation, almost like the startled expression of a person recognizing someone she knew or remembered vaguely. Her face was framed by a wild mane of flaxen blonde hair so soft and thin it looked like the wispy strands on ripening corn. The girl smiled what was not really a smile, but a simple twitch of the lips, then before I could step back onto my feet she put out her gloved hand as if to raise me up from the unbearable indignity of my prostration. Her body, which was slim and firm and immensely *white*, was so close to me I could smell it. Then she did something so unexpectedly curious and inexplicable that to this day I can find no explanation for it. In order to offer me her hand, to restore my balance as it seemed, the girl pulled off her white glove so that it was a small naked hand she placed on my bare arm. A moment of wordless panic like a sudden seizure of the heart overtook me. I tried to move backward but without much success and I felt the hand, soft yet strong in its grasp, lift me to my feet, and whether from the glove or her own person I shall never know, came a strange, powerful fragrance I had never smelled before, a scent stronger than the perfume of a rose, yet sharper than the bouquet of the freshest blossom I have ever smelled. I looked up into her face. The girl who was neither ugly nor pretty, but whose face was something strange, unexpected, and luminous like the glare of blinding light, was smiling down at me with the gentlest of expressions.

She must have spoken then some words of comfort, words that were an impulsive movement toward an apology for her family's intrusion into what was after all the shopping emporium for us, the black dispossessed and the eternally humiliated. I have really no idea what she said. Like her father who now waited impatiently for her to join them, the man whose language I could not really have understood, the girl spoke a language that was meaningless to me except what the eyes and the pressure of her hand conveyed. Her eyes seemed to fill the space between us with a flashing blue radiance that echoed in my blood with the sound of anarchy and the dimmest recognition of the momentous gesture of sympathy one human being can feel for another, a kind of benediction that transforms the moment of contact into one of revelation.

From the Zulus came the low murmur of discontent like the hum of bees, a kind of whispered curse, an intake of breath accompanied by fear and horror at the touch of white skin upon black skin. However, even before we had had time to digest and assimilate the meaning of the drama, the girl, her parents, and her sister, had all resumed their slow procession into the Indian store.

I had no wish to wait to see them reemerge from the shop. For a second I stood upon the steps in stunned incomprehension, hugging my arm where the white girl had placed her hand as though I had developed a stigma that nothing, no prayer, no memory eraser, certainly not my father's warning, could finally remove, and I ran down the remainder of the steps to join my mother where she waited in the courtyard of the shop.

After my death, many people reading this memoir will consider this a not very significant episode and will be inclined to see it as the product of the rambling mind of a gallows bird, which will add very little that might help to illumine the nature of the predicament into which I ultimately fell, yet I cannot help but feel that there is something in that first encounter with the white girl that marked me for life, a psychic wound so permanently opened that when it came to telling my story to Dr. Emile Dufré, I was reluctant to narrate the events relating to this incident. Why did I withhold what was, on the surface, a not very remarkable occurrence? Again and again Dufré asked me to relate to him the very first time that I saw a white woman, and again and again I could only repeat, "At the Lutheran Seminary. One of my master's wives." And though I could recall the incident with exact details, I said nothing about the white girl at the Mzimba Shopping Center. I suppressed the incident altogether. Why? I suggest that an answer to that question would open for Emile Dufré new and interesting areas for investigation.

10

A few months before my last year at the Lutheran Seminary, rumors began to travel from the white town of Mzimba that the whole village of Manzimhlophe was to be moved to an area fifty miles inland to make way for a new white settlement. At first, people did not believe what they heard. After all, these were Zulu ancestral lands where generations upon generations had buried their dead, and the blood of Zulu warriors, long before their final conquest by the white men, had mingled with the red soil of the valleys and the Zulu plains. But when the Bantu commissioner, a tall, thin man with a long, hawklike nose dividing a pair of green eyes, arrived from Eshowe, bearing papers signed with indelible government ink, there was no longer any doubt as to the seriousness of the situation. Without plans and without organization, a few reckless people spoke of the need to resist, of the need to fight back if necessary, but there was little time to unite our people into a strong resistance force.

The day the soldiers came to the village with bulldozers, people were standing around in little knots, watching with disbelief their huts and cattle enclosures quickly razed to the ground, the little they owned being loaded on military trucks. Some of the soldiers were not content to leave it at that. In a show of force that was entirely unprovoked, they went about breaking up clusters of individuals who silently watched the remorseless destruction of their ancient village; those who murmured complaints were quickly beaten up or arrested for obstruction; a few faces were slapped, and it was not long before the people were forced to scatter at the sound of shots being fired repeatedly above their heads in an obvious attempt to frighten them. My father had moved the entire family to my maternal uncle's village twenty miles away from Mzimba in order to avoid attempts to corral us with the rest of the people who were to be dumped into a government-protected village, but all my relatives, old and young, had returned to watch the soldiers armed with rifles lay devastation to the mud huts and the cattle kraals.

Two weeks later, when my father died suddenly without any warning, my mother in her bitter lamentations claimed that grief and despair, not old age, had killed him.

The death also signaled the final split-up of the family, with some traveling further inland, others like my mother deciding to try their fortunes in the big city of Durban. It was as if the thread that had held us together like a bunch of straw had simply been unraveled. At a stroke, everything fell apart.

II

When I had finished telling Dufré about Mzimba, speaking, as I normally did, very rapidly and somewhat disjointedly, I could tell that despite his heroic show of cheerful satisfaction he was somewhat disappointed with the narrative, especially its lack of relevance to the specific area of his investigation, its lack of graphic detail. I had noticed that throughout the interview he had given the impression of an inquirer who craved for a particularly damaging piece of information and what he had received was simply a bland relating of not very interesting facts. The disappointment showed on the doctor's aging face, which looked more tired than ever. Sorrow, frustration were on it, the look of a thwarted animal like a hungry mongrel who has been prevented from fastening his fangs on a juicy bone. This led me to the sad conclusion about Dufré; the impression I have begun to form of the Swiss doctor is of a person who, despite many periodic expressions of sympathy for me personally, has not entirely given up the notion that yes, I am guilty, that somehow I must be a highly dangerous sex maniac to have been apprehended and convicted. In this respect he is no different from every white person who, brainwashed by government and police propaganda, by the sensationalistic and highly embellished portrayals in the newspapers, believes I am a compulsive rapist who goes around making attacks on innocent white women. I regret this very much, that Dufré with whom I have formed a strong bond is no different from the others. When he saw Veronica Slater in the witness box, he saw a seductive woman, no doubt, a dazzlingly pretty one, certainly, but a young woman who did not deserve such a cruel fate. That is what Dufré thought. He did not question the facts of the case, only the form of punishment. Dufré thinks that the punishment may be extreme, of course, but the crime was also, undeniably, brutal. His solicitous manner toward me does not fool me.

Of course, given the nature of all the allegations against me, given the constant attempts to smear and discredit me in court, and given, finally, the conviction and the sentence, all of which created the impression of an impartial assessment of guilt, Dufré's attitude may seem more than justified. But is it really? Why believe the word of the girl against mine, for example? Except for the *whiteness* of her skin, a color that has caused more trouble and unhappiness in the world than the color of any other skin, what particular claim to virtue can this girl be supposed to have? Indeed, Dufré's willingness to believe my accusers more than he feels inclined to accept my own word in self-defense smacks of prejudice, to say the very least. In consequence, I feel toward him a certain amount of reserve.

There. The truth is out. I cannot help it. To the criminologist, to Emile Dufré and the rest of his brotherhood, I feel I am nothing more than a specimen of a socially malfunctioning individual whose name may yet figure in the growing annals of sexual crimes. Of my actual personality, of my roots and the meaning of my past, of the subtle and complex emotions that the merest recollection of the landscape of my childhood is still capable of evoking, Dufré is woefully ignorant. And yet! And yet every day I look forward to his visits. The need to make wild and inexcusable confessions to someone with nothing better to do than listen has become stronger with each passing day as we move inexorably toward the day of execution. Dufré, I have found, is a good listener. After the brief interlude in which both of us give ourselves to a moment of silent reflection, I conclude the recollections of my childhood, a time of my life that has begun to seem, even to me, unreal, fantastical, partaking only of a false sunlit glow of legend. "It was, all the same, the happiest time of my life," I tell Dufré.

"I'm sure it was," Dufré says sympathetically. "But can you say why this was such a particularly happy time for you?"

"I'm not sure I can explain it, Dr. Dufré." It occurs to

me that at the time I was growing up I did not consider myself particularly happy. Perhaps a child does not value childhood very greatly. At the time I was growing up I certainly did not value mine. Perhaps a child is impressed only by the general tedium of growing up, by the necessity of following rules and regulations that for the most part seem to have neither rhyme nor reason, but, for all that, rules and regulations that are invariably imposed with unrelenting severity by adults. In my own case, these rules had not caused much undue suffering, it is true. Yet it is a peculiar admission to make that at the time I had not even wanted this happy childhood or any other childhood for that matter. I had simply wanted to be grown-up, to be a mature individual, possessing unlimited opportunities for shaping my own life and destiny, according to my own efforts and possibilities. In this object I might have failed in the end, but even the failures I wanted to be my own. Among the failures I include the English girl, naturally. She, too, was a mistake and yet I can say *that* mistake was truly mine. After all, it was I who chose to run after the girl: out of my own inclination, with no other purpose in mind than to discover the sexual reasons for the white man's singular protectiveness toward his womenfolk, I gradually conceived the idea of attaining knowledge of some willing white woman.

At first this idea was no more than a vague intention, but later it acquired the fatal attractiveness of an ungovernable passion. When the English girl finally appeared out of nowhere, bearing her wealth of sexual plenitude and very little else, if I may say so, she seemed to have been put in my path in order to answer a great and overwhelming need. From that day onward, until our hasty copulation in the bungalow, I followed her everywhere. I watched her constantly. Whenever the opportunity presented itself, I haunted her path. At night, in my base and intolerable lust, I dreamed of her, and in my dreams I touched her soft skin and smooth hair. (In reality, as I was later to find out, the skin was neither so soft nor the hair so smooth as I had at first imagined.) All the same, the girl eventually became a kind of sickness for me. Was it probable that someone like Dufré, with his immense skill and powers of analysis, could succeed in uncovering something in my background that would provide a clue to my behavior, something that could endow with meaning my choice of this girl or the passion that with each glimpse of her shadowy form I conceived for her; some defect of personality, perhaps, some mental distortion that would indicate the culmination of a particular history of mental aberration and sexual disorder? As an educated man, I know this is the object of Dufré's inquiry: to find a clue, to acquire the missing link. As though to confirm this, Dufré suddenly leans forward and addresses me with startling intensity: "You see, Mr. Sibiya, in our experience we have found that many people who commit crimes of this nature are the product of a defective and unhappy childhood."

"My childhood was not defective, Dr. Dufré."

"In every respect? How can you be sure?"

"My childhood was quite normal by any standards."

For the first time since we began our conversation this morning, Dufré looks irritated, the corners of his mouth sag unattractively, the twitch on the side of his face becomes more pronounced. He takes off his glasses to give them a brief polish.

"My friend, if you'll forgive my saying so, truly speaking we can state with a fairly absolute certainty of being right that no childhood is ever quite normal." With a certain crispness in the tone of his voice, his words also carry the tinge of a rebuke as though the doctor of mental illness has been personally affronted.

Unreasonably I persist, "I can remember nothing abnormal about mine."

"Really?" Dufré interjects, unable to keep the sarcasm out of his voice. "Well, try."

"To what purpose, doctor, when I have only a few days to live? What good will it do me to think about the flaws in my personality when my execution is all that I need to look forward to?"

The allusion to the subject of my imminent execution never ceases to embarrass Dufré. At its mention, you can see his brow darken with anxiety and depression, his lips tighten with internal discomfort. "There you go again," Dufré sighs. "Death! Hanging! If you don't mind my saying so, Mr. Sibiya, even granting the nature of your predicament, I find your fascination with death slightly puzzling."

"I'm sorry, doctor, but as a famous French poet once put it, 'To be born is to have commenced to die.'"

"The words of a useless French poet!" Dufré explodes. "I'm surprised that someone in your place should've spent so much time reading the works of a decadent French poet like Gautier. Let me tell you something, my friend. These sentiments you repeat to me with so much confidence were uttered by a European poet whose race had already begun its journey toward death and dissolution. Happily, your civilization is only at its brightest morning. It is a flower, a pure flame, which burns the strongest for not having been clouded by so much murder and perversion as we have seen in Europe!" (Dada Amin would have enjoyed that!) "Your civilization is at the very beginning of a long and cheerful struggle that must be waged with vigor and intelligence. Of all people, you should be an optimist, Mr. Sibiya!"

Optimist? What have I got to be optimistic about? I wanted to shout, "What about my execution!" until I noticed Dufré's eyes gazing at me with a certain nervous caution and very prudently I decided to avoid alluding to a subject that gives my illustrious visitor so much pain and discomfort. All the same, I cannot help reflecting sourly that even in misfortune the Europeans must lay claim to some form of superior woe. Once it was against the virtue and intelligence of their genius that we could not compete, now it is the formidable nature of their spiritual crisis that we cannot easily match. Theirs, it is claimed with barely concealed satisfaction, is a great struggle, surpassing anything yet known to man, and if they should die of this rapidly worsening disease, they at least take deep satisfaction in the fact that we can never know the exact dimensions of their anguish. Patronizing, you might say. All the same, I do not think the good doctor meant to be unkind. There is something altogether admirable in the conduct of this man, so grave, so patient, so calmly persistent.

"That is why," Dr. Dufré quietly confides, "even in your case, Mr. Sibiya, faced as you are with imminent annihilation, we must talk only of the part you play in the never-ceasing flow of life, not of death."

This is the kind of eloquence I have never been able to resist. Even though I can tell there is something strangely incongruous, given my current predicament, about the reference to the "never-ceasing flow of life," appeals of this sort to first principles, to the eternal laws of man's existence, of his constant, indeed, uncheckable regeneration, are sufficiently persuasive to overcome my resistance.

All the same, sometimes I experience a momentary doubt; but Dufré remains impregnable in his faith in what we Africans would yet become. This patience, this dogged singlemindedness, I know, built whole civilizations and mighty empires, but to be the object of its passion, I confess, can only reduce the victim to a state of extreme fatigue.

Nevertheless, there is something wholly admirable about Dufré's manner, always grave, patient, and courteous, his sad owlish eyes flashing behind the rimless glasses, the soft-fleshed mouth and hollow cheekbones suggesting an aborted sensuality that has yielded to a thoughtful contemplation of life.

Dufré presents a picture of quiet tenacity coupled with obdurate intelligence. He will not easily give up the purpose of this mission, which, as he has frequently indicated to me, is to compile the full portrait of an "African rapist," whose exploits have captured the imagination of the entire "civilized world." He is the perfect scholar, tireless in his pursuit of "facts," rigorous in the sifting and testing of hypotheses.

"Look, Dr. Dufré," I say to him. "I appreciate what you're trying to do. It's even remotely possible that a case like mine will enrich the rapidly growing science of human behavior. Only you must believe me when I say I'm not accustomed to talking so much about myself. As a rule, I'm rather a shy person."

"You? Shy?" Dufré smiles disbelievingly. "Please, Mr. Sibiya, I hope you'll allow me to lodge a minor objection to your formulation. Your past behavior does not in any way accord with that of a shy and retiring personality. Consider the facts for a moment as they emerged from your trial. For weeks, for months, you place yourself in every location where she is sure to pass. No risk is too great for you where this lady is concerned. You'll please note, I refrain from applying to your conduct the description the prosecution had no difficulty in employing to characterize your behavior. 'Hounded' was the word the prosecution used. They said you 'hounded' the poor girl. On the beach you placed yourself in such a manner as to obtain the maximum view of her sunbathing. In the end you endeavored to get as near her body as decency, to say nothing of your peculiar race laws, would permit. And now you wish me to believe that your fatal handicap is unusual shyness? Really, Mr. Sibiya, I do not wish to sound unduly skeptical!"

I know what Dufré is doing. He is trying to provoke me into losing my temper. At such an unguarded moment I might be moved into making rash disclosures. All the same, knowing this does not make me any more immune to anger at this sudden crude attack than knowing the symptom of a disease can prevent one from feeling the effects of the disease.

"All right! All right!" I say to him impatiently. "Only

it wasn't at all like that! In court, I tried to explain how it happened but no one would believe me. How many times must I tell you the girl invited sexual attention? Don't you believe me when I say whatever else happened, that girl wanted it to happen? Right from the beginning I could tell she wanted it as much as I did. Though neither of us spoke, those meetings at the beach took on the form of rendez-vous. She waited for my arrival each day as keenly as I looked forward to hers. It was in her eyes, it was all over her face. A pact is what we had entered into, a silent con-spiracy. Even on the day of the incident, although she could see me hanging about her front yard, she still left the door of the bungalow open! And what of the stripping, eh, doc-tor? How do you explain the striptease act? Right there before me, with the front door wide open, removing every bit of clothing until she was standing in full view with nothing but bare powder on her back! Can you explain that?"

Dufré smiles as he always does, sympathetically, with grave respect for my viewpoint, but it is obvious he does not believe me. "What about the time you followed her to a concert at the Durban City Hall? For days you had been lying in wait for her outside her bungalow, watching her comings and goings at all hours of the day and night! An-other time you followed her to the door of a private house where a party was in progress. Although this was a white area practically out of bounds to natives, you had no hesita-tion in following her to this house where you then climbed a fence, which enabled you to observe what admittedly struck you as very strange goings-on?"

Pausing to examine my face in obvious satisfaction,

Dufré beams a smile at me. "Well? Is what you did the behavior of a normal native male in a country where the race laws are as strict as in your own?" As usual, Dufré gives the impression of an investigator who suspects there is more to the story than what he is told. He taps his pad musingly with a pen. He hums a tune. His manner has also subtly changed as though he feels that he has finally driven me into a tight corner.

"I admit there was an element of an obsession in my behavior," I finally explode. "I confessed it in court, I never denied it, but what no one is ready to admit, apparently, is that Veronica's behavior, too, was very odd, to say the very least." Dufré smiles faintly at my use of the girl's first name, but I ignore the obvious implication of his smile.

"Really you must believe me, doctor, when I say even the times when I followed her to public places she was very much aware of it; I might even say it was with her encouragement I did so. I know no one will believe it, but when I did follow her I had not the faintest doubt that she recognized me from our silent meetings on the beach. On several occasions when I came across her, I had the curious impression that she even smiled in recognition.

"I can't very well explain it. Even during that party scene, when the whole group of them, from what perverted motive I cannot say, seemed to have deliberately left the curtains open for any passerby to obtain a fleeting view of what was surely an orgy in progress, I had a distinct feeling that each time her face cut across my view, that whenever I caught a glimpse of her embracing a man, that she was aware that somewhere outside that house, silent, petrified but enthralled, a slave to habit, I was watching her, that somewhere behind that fence I was holding vigil. Each time she turned toward that window, she would pause for a second with her naked body in full view and give the sketchiest impression of a smile. It was as if she could not live another day without the sustaining need that there was a 'native' somewhere who desired her to distraction (or shall we say to destruction!); a black man who in his impossible dream of gaining possession of her was prepared to throw his life away in a stupid wager against the state, against Fate itself. For in my lust for her, Veronica must have recognized the force of her own social existence, the image of her own sexual powers; in the ability to arouse the inextinguishable desire in others, she must have obtained confirmation of her own immense and undeniable necessity in our small corrupted universe. Seen in that light, both the girl and I were hooked. We were both obsessed with the other unadmitted presence. To her, I dare say, I was as much of a drug as she was to me, the ultimate mirror in which she saw reflected the power of her sex and her race.''

''Bravo!'' Dufré applauded, clapping his hands, his sallow face radiant with delight. ''I had no idea how penetrating your mind could be. Given a chance, you would make an excellent analyst of sexual motivation.'' But these explosions of mirth in Dufré, of unexpected humor and lightness of touch, are few and far between. Most of the time Dufré leans back in his chair, his face gravely serene behind his flashing rimless glasses, the crown of his domelike head as smooth as a baby's bottom. He listens intently without ceasing to doodle on the open notebook placed on his lap. Dufré's eyes are always sleepy but watchful, alert. Despite the impression of somnolence, his tired face also possesses

an expression of avid curiosity, mocking and skeptical yet
frankly expectant, as though he hopes to hear more damaging revelations. This complacency always makes me furious.
Nothing is more offensive to me than the distant objectivity
in a social scientist who is more concerned with proving
hypotheses than with discovering the true character of one
man's passion for another human being.

"I see. You don't believe me?" I say angrily.

"The court did not believe you!" Dufré counters.

Outside my cell door I can hear African prisoners singing freedom songs in loud defiant voices: *"Indod,"* *"em-
nyama,"* *"u-Vorster!,"* *"Thina Sizwe!"* Dufré, too, is listening. Suddenly, while both of us listen, we can hear feet
running, the sounds of slaps and swearing. There is a loud
crash against the door of my cell and a voice is heard pleading yet defiant at the same time, an African voice. *"My Kron,
laat ek mos jou vertel!"*

"Voetsek, jou ma se gat!"

"Please, baas, my *ma hoor,* I didn't do it!"

"Bloody liar, I'll make you eat your *kaffer* shit! You
hear?" And the blows! We can hear the hard thump of fists
against a defenseless body, the dismal sound of bones crushing against a concrete wall. These beatings go on and on,
every day, every week. I try to shut my ears against the
screams and the thunder of fists and the singing of the
sjambok, but it is no good. Only when the beatings are over
and the bolts in the doors of every cell have been shot home
is there the unmistakable sound of voices, first humming in
unison, then as though an open channel were building up
into an ocean of sound. Voices begin singing, singing, singing until the entire block of the enclosed prison echoes with

the amazing sound of hundreds of prisoners' voices, chanting, *"The Nation will step on you, Dr. Vorster!"* And the swelling crescendo of *"Thwal 'umthwalo, sigoduke!"*

While these freedom songs are being sung, no one moves, no one talks, even the wind seems completely still as though the world were listening breathlessly to some universal chant of freedom. Only those who understand the words are moved to join in until the very prison walls seem to shake and vibrate with the volume of voices united in the sentiment of their unspoken demand for liberty.

12

While we were listening to this uproar, there was a sudden jangling of keys at my cell door. The heavy iron bolt was moved to one side, and very slowly the massive steel door creaked on its hinges as it was pushed back. Before anyone could step into the door, a flood of white light, so sharp and glaring in its intensity that both Dufré and I had to blink in the immensity of its whiteness, poured into the gloomy cell. It was a light that in its harshness brought the hint of the outside world beyond the prison walls, the sharp-edged clarity of houses and trees and the physical landscape drawn against the overwhelming blueness of the sky. We could smell the outdoors, too, an acrid, burning, smoky odor of trees and buildings frying under the mid-October sun, but for all that, the air from outside seemed a whole lot fresher than the slightly damp musty staleness of the cell. And the sound. We could hear from a distance the constant din of a city chafing its muscle against the day's industry.

Then, while I briefly contemplated the patch of blue sky through a door that was still being pushed open, the tall figure of Col. A. C. Van Rooyen, blurred like an unfocused picture but suggestive of the immense bulk of the man, abruptly filled the doorway. I was as startled by this apparition as I had often been startled by the sudden appearance of the English girl on the beach, by the violent disruption of light of which the white skin was capable, as if it could only succeed in repelling the sunlight, not in absorbing it; black skin, no doubt, was more absorbent, more dense and luxuriant. And yet it was not that Van Rooyen was that delicately white. More reddish brown, I would say. Grave, powerful, and subtly menacing, he hovered above us, casting a strong hawkish glance, first at the Swiss doctor, then at me.

"Everything going okay, *Meneer* Dufré?" Dufré attempted to rise.

"Very well, *Herr* Commander!"

And Van Rooyen, watching the Swiss struggling to his feet, intercepted him.

"Please, don't trouble yourself, *Dokter*." He was in his khaki uniform, which was always starched, as stainless as Sheffield steel. In one hand he carried a baton with a steel shiny knob with which he kept slapping the open palm of one hand. The light behind him made the crown of his closely cropped hair bristle like the mane of a lion, but I could see nothing of his face except a blur of white light, the liquid gray eyes, and the toothbrush mustache carefully trimmed. Glancing in my direction, the man who was the terror of Durban Central Prison nodded approvingly.

"Keep at him, Meneer Dufré. Keep at him. Let him tell you everything. You will be surprised what kind of stories some of these boys can tell you." He looked rather benevolently at me, I thought, then half-jokingly suggested, "And if a glass of brandy will facilitate his memory, Meneer Dufré, I'm prepared to overlook prison regulations and have a bottle sent down to you."

I thought for a while with a sudden, unreasoning alarm that Dufré would spurn the offer but after a quick imploring glance at the visitor's perspiring face, now faintly lit by an appreciative grin, I knew he would not be so foolish. The psychologist must have seen the desperate prayer in my face. He was quick to accept. "Yes, perhaps, that is very kind of you, Commandant. Perhaps a little of *something* might help to ease the strain."

"Very well." Van Rooyen nodded. "I'll give instructions. A nip of brandy and two glasses. Okay, Sibiya?" He made a rather grim attempt at a smile, but as usual the result was disconcerting.

"Thank you, Big Baas!"

Since my arrival at Durban Central Prison I had never seen the Prison Commandant smile; once I had heard him laugh, if you could call a high-pitched, mirthless hyena screech a laugh. At the time I had been detailed to scrub and polish his Spartan office in the left wing of the prison. While trying to proceed with my task in which I was considerably hampered by Van Rooyen's constant pacing up and down the floor, a pale-faced messenger burst into the office. "Commandant!" he blurted out. "Yes. What is it, Maurie?" Van Rooyen growled. "I fear something terrible has happened!"

Van Rooyen looked up. "Something terrible? What the hell are you talking about, man! Come on, speak up!" Then something I can only describe as a kind of illumination flashed across the face of the Police Commandant. "My wife?" he said almost ecstatically. "It is my wife!" The messenger nodded. The white boy was close to tears. "Shortly after you left this morning, Mrs. Van Rooyen was found in the bathroom by the *kaffermeidjie* hanging by the belt of her dressing gown. The *meidjie* says she was as naked as the day she was born." There was an awful stillness in the office during which I made a desperate effort to efface my presence as far as that was possible. In the shock of this communication, the white man had forgotten about me. Or perhaps it was true what every African believes, that white people never regard the blacks as human beings with eyes and ears, but more like flies on the walls. It was then, unbelievingly, I heard Van Rooyen burst into laughter. "That *skellum* whore has gone and done it at last!" he cried, half sobbed, half crowed, his monumental hand grasping at the top of the chair. "Done it!" he cried again. "Goddammit, Maurie! This calls for a celebration, man!" I was astounded. Was it a white man's joke? I saw the messenger hesitate while Van Rooyen produced a flask of brandy and two glasses, into which he poured two fingers of cognac, handing one to the bewildered young man. "*Kom, kom*, Maurie," his face flushed with excitement, Van Rooyen urged the young man to take a drink. "To my wife, Katie, the biggest whore who ever walked the face of the earth. May she rot in hell!" He lifted his glass but he never drank it. Instead, he suddenly collapsed and he wept like a baby. I left as quietly as possible while the other man threw his arm around the Prison Commander, trying to comfort him. As I say, that was the first time I had heard Van Rooyen laugh, or cry for that matter.

Before turning to go, Van Rooyen turned to the Zurich doctor and said rather gently, "He's a good boy, Sibiya. I'm sure he'll cooperate fully with you, Dr. Dufré." Then thinking it rather strange that he should pay such a compliment to one condemned to die, he quickly added, "It's a pity he developed a taste for white women, otherwise he wouldn't be waiting to hang now, eh Sibiya?"

"*Ja, Meneer*," I said. After all, it was the truth. The English girl had been my undoing. When the cell door had been bolted once more, and Dufré and I were left to ponder for a minute the motive for the Commandant's visit, I realized with a certain amount of embarrassment that I had indeed become the prized poodle of this wretched, miserable man, whose work promised no escape from a life of obscurity, whose wife had been, according to more than one newspaper, a failed concert singer, inclined to the bottle, with a suggestion of worse weaknesses of character. No doubt, Van Rooyen was a sour man, even a cruel man, but since foreign journalists and international observers had begun descending like vultures on Durban Central on account of my celebrated case, and Van Rooyen's pictures and interviews had begun appearing in the newspapers with astonishing regularity, his attitude toward me had subtly changed. During these interviews, in which he even managed to say some kind things about me, Van Rooyen was given to making lengthy statements about the problems of law and order in South Africa. He expounded on the political climate, especially the unthinking hostility of the international community, in which dedicated men like himself were obliged to function. He mentioned the soaring crime rate at home, especially crimes of sexual violence; he pointed me out as a tragic example of what white liberal education can do to simple, good-natured natives, stimulating as it was surely bound to do, not only a love of a western style of living but also an unbridled desire for white women. I saw one of these interviews in a yellowing copy of the *Daily News* in which my captor concluded by observing that the natives, left to their tribal environment, were all right, their morals were even superior to those of some whites, but given a smattering of education, they became spoiled and thought of themselves as equals of white men. He concluded by citing as an example the rapid increase of incidents of assault on white women. This, Van Rooyen said, was the necessary and tragic consequence of the ill-conceived projects of social uplift, which white liberals fondly hoped would transform the natives into something like white men. He summed up by issuing a warning to white ladies, some of whom, he regretted to say, were in the habit of displaying themselves in the most provocative manner in front of black servants; it was time everyone recognized, Van Rooyen said, that we were here dealing not with normal men but creatures who were little above animals.

13

Van Rooyen was apparently not the only one to believe in the corrupting power of western education. Many Africans, especially in the countryside, held similar ideas. My father, for example. Against this general background of distrust and fatalistic disapproval, my mother's untested faith makes her stand out as something of an inspired radical and innovator.

I remember her good spirits that day we traveled to the white town of Mzimba to make purchases for my first adventure into the domains of western science and learning.

In the rickety bus that carried us to town, chatting happily with other excited passengers in the manner in which our people become instant friends as soon as they start on a journey, she laughed a great deal that morning, pride obvious in the radiance of her face. Against the velvet black of her skin, her milk-white teeth flashed like beacons in the night. When she laughed, her breasts, naked above the cow-leather skirt, a little heavier than one would have expected from her slim figure (to this day I can still remember how the older women disapproved of my mother's so-called skinniness), skipped up and down like young does and bounced like pears on the branch of a pear tree as she shook with laughter. She was aware of the attention she was attracting and, of course, she reveled in it. She was young again, her laughter, her sighs, her movements must have been full of provocations for the men; and, to my discomfiture, she confided to everyone within hearing about the future of her son who was soon to enter school. To hear her talk, you would think no one had ever been to school before, and what profound transformation of character and mind she hoped schooling would produce it was only possible to guess at. No doubt, she was convinced that an encounter, however brief, with books, would confer upon her offspring awesome powers of the occult, an almost miraculous ability to manipulate the universe at will. "Can you just see him," she asked, laughing, "sitting behind those tables the white people use for writing on at Mzimba, driving his pen across the white page like some of those clerks you see at the government office! A real devil Ndi is going to be with a pen, you wait and see!" Coquettish, very beautiful in her headgear embroidered with beads, she put her arm around me, drawing me into the warmth of her hot, clammy armpit and inclining her head a little she laughed, curling her tongue inside her mouth like a snake. Such fine teeth she had, and the eyes, dark and sparkling, added to the mystery of her allure.

I felt ashamed at her obvious foolishness, but I was also dazzled and pleased by her beauty, and when I thought of the school I was about to enter, I felt a little humbled by the enormity of the undertaking. What would I do with all that school learning? Be a teacher, a doctor, a clerk, or would I perhaps write great books that school-going children in our village had sometimes shown to me? I had no idea. Every turning seemed to hide new unexpected vistas, every corner seemed to hold infinite possibilities as well as immense dangers, and I was not reassured by the comments I heard from other passengers: "Well, you know what these young people are like when they get all that white man's learning! The moment they're able to say ' 'scuse me' like white people, they want to sell us like so many useless cattle!"

A woman laughed jeeringly: "I once saw a citywoman at Mzimba, one of those clever ones who have gone to school. She had a mouth painted red and she was smoking a cigarette. I said to her, are you not afraid your mouth will catch fire?"

"What did she answer you?" mother asked.

"She said, shut your mouth, you pagan woman! That's what she said. She called me *iqaba!* You wait and see. Your own son will call you *iqaba* one of these days when he has learned to say ' 'scuse me' like a white man and can smoke a cigarette from the corner of his mouth."

The man who had spoken first laughed and said to my mother, "Even if he calls you a pagan, I hope he will never have to paint his mouth red like those city whores!"

This kind of talk was demoralizing. It awakened all the latent fears my father's warning had already bred in me. Thus it happened that instead of stimulating great joy within me, the trip to Mzimba and the rest of the preparations that followed stirred up a deep sense of gloom and foreboding as though going to school was the first signal of some unknown disaster, a tragedy that was now only beginning, slowly, to unfold. Clairvoyant, you might say, in the light of what later came to pass, but I am not convinced that my fate was quite so inevitable. In a confused sort of way, I sensed, too, with very little experience to guide me, that the path on which I was now launched would mean at some future date a complete break with the family, with the clan and with all that had sustained my spirit up to now. Henceforth I would remain one of the Sibiyas only in name, but in every way that mattered I would become a "white man," as my half brother, Sipho, had once gravely told me. "Look at these Zulus who have gone to school," he had snorted. "Have you not seen the way they walk, sideways like a crab? It is the white man's knowledge that does it to them. They say you can go mad just from knowing too much book. Like that man in the village who stares at a piece of paper full of dots before singing something."

That trip to Mzimba was itself the beginning of a process of initiation in which I saw myself as a young man setting out on a long and tortuous journey, beset by dangers and uncertainty. For this adventure I needed my battle dress in the form of school uniforms and implements of war such as books, slates, notebooks, and pens. Standing at the long counter of Saloojee's Trading Store at Mzimba, the articles lying pell-mell about us before my mother made up her mind what to purchase and what to reject, I sensed once again the importance of the occasion, the solemnity with which everyone treated the news of my impending recruitment to the ranks of the small but significant population of school-going children.

As our fellow passengers predicted that morning, the end has not been a happy one; not life but death, not wisdom but foolishness. Today I sit in this death cell, awaiting execution, because having gone to school I was no longer content with what I was. My hungers, my frustrations, my pride and ambition led me into thorny paths and finally into the noose. The Zulus have a saying: *Hamba juba, bokuhlutha phambili!* "Fly on wood-dove, they will pluck your feathers where you alight." Durban, it would seem, was the destination where my feathers were finally to be plucked!

14

Durban was another world altogether, vast, incomprehensible, completely unexpected. My father dead, his family scattered in different parts of the country, and Mzimba as far away as if it had been part of another universe, mother had chosen to make a fresh start in the big city of Durban, a busy seaport with its gigantic cargo ships and passenger liners, its oil and sugar refineries, its colorful flower gardens, its rickshaws, its vastly spaced streets, its mosques, and its dark crowded slums.

On arrival in the big city of Durban my mother had

immediately shown her resourcefulness by finding an un-tenanted shack in Cato Manor, the sprawling, fetid, black slum five miles outside the center of the city. The tin shan-ties of Cato Manor clung precariously as if for dear life to the hillsides and slopes overlooking a stream called Mkhumbane, whose greenish slimy waters flowed eastward and southward on its sluggish journey toward the Indian Ocean, embracing to its already heavily polluted bosom all the scum and filth of innumerable shacks without proper sewage, without proper toilets or plumbing, on hot days as unbearably hot as overheated ovens, on rainy days as leaky as open sieves. Many of these shacks and lean-tos were owned by Indian landlords, but these Indians, existing un-certainly between the poor mass of black people and the richer white population, were themselves now threatened with eviction in order to make room for more white habita-tion. So were the Africans, of course. The location to the west, with its rows upon rows of neat, terraced houses, firmer, more durable than the fragile corrugated iron hov-els into which mother and I had moved, had already excited the envy of many privileged white citizens. The location was also under the axe. *Ilanga,* the newspaper for black people, argued with considerable force that rather than destroy houses already in existence, more were needed to accommodate people from the slums of Cato Manor, but its words fell on deaf ears. Just as at Mzimba, here, too, the whites were preparing to dislodge the indigenous inhabi-tants in order to take over the best parts of the land.

In Cato Manor, African women lived mainly by brew-ing an illicit concoction called *skokiaan,* which was often laced with methylated spirit to give it an extra kick. This

dangerous and mind-destroying brew was then served daily
to black workers, who, evening after evening, as soon as
they left work, flocked to their favorite *shebeens,* where they
thirstily imbibed the stuff in a vain effort, some said, to
forget the misery of pass-raids, the misery of unpaid rents,
the misery of uncompleted rental charges. The drinking
went on until the small hours of the morning. After the
drinking there were the fights, often very violent fights,
some even ending in deaths. Between the shacks, along the
darkened passageways, women shamelessly offered themselves to men, who took them greedily, standing them up,
or leaning them against the wall.

At first mother resisted the repeated advice from other
women to move in on the illicit liquor trade herself. Ma-
Mlambo, a dominant figure in our neighborhood, was the
first to call at our twin-roomed shack. There were others to
follow her.

Very black in complexion, with eyes set so wide apart
and so far back on the side of her face they seemed to be
staring sideways like a chameleon's, Ma-Mlambo was
reputed to have once been a successful diviner. That had
been a very long time ago, before she had come to live in
the big city. In Durban, she had quickly found that city
Africans had a different cast of mind from what she had
expected; more skeptical, less easy to convince than country
people, they did not flock to her in large numbers to learn
whose powerful medicine was responsible for the failure of
their business, who was casting a spell over their sick daughter, or who was attempting to break up their household.
Defeated but unbowed, Ma-Mlambo had turned to *shebeen-*
running.

"I hear you come from Mzimba?" Ma-Mlambo said to my mother that morning, speaking without introduction and without much ceremony. "This is not exactly Mzimba, you know. This is Mdubane. Here, when you run out of money, you will soon find that no one cares a tuppence what happens to you! This is a cutthroat world, child of my people. Coolies! Kaffirs! Boesmans!" She shot out a stream of brown saliva at her feet. "They're all the same! Sharks who will skin you alive for the sake of a chance to put their two fingers inside your purse."

My mother grumbled at the word "kaffir," but Ma-Mlambo merely snorted at her. "What do you want me to call them? What I say is true. *Amakhafula!*" She repeated the word. "That's what they are! After all, they live off the crumbs from the white man's table, don't they, and the white man wipes his backside on them. What do you call such people? Listen, I'll give you some advice. Work for yourself. Brewing is the thing here. No matter how many of us go into this business there is never enough stuff to satisfy the thirsty men from the factories and the docks. People will drink anything to forget their troubles!"

My mother said she had never heard of people brewing in order to sell. In the countryside, women brewed traditional beer regularly in order to offer it as hospitality to those who called in for a chat or even strangers who stopped for a gourd to quench their thirst on their way to distant lands. I suppose outrage and disbelief were written all over my mother's face because Ma-Mlambo, sensing disapproval, was not slow to move into the attack. "No need for you to turn up your nose like that because things are not what they used to be. What do you expect? This is

a big city, nothing is free here. Mdubane is not your countryside, where people chat all day under the shade of the
mimosa!" Pausing only to take a pinch of snuff, she went
on. "So what do you aim to do? It's only fair to ask. You
want to be a maid in Berea?"

In the event my mother did not become a maid in
Berea, but she did the nearest thing to being a maid: she
took in washing for white people. On Mondays she went on
her rounds, collecting the dirty laundry, which she brought
home to wash in a big tub in the front yard. Watched by half
a dozen squatting women, she emptied the laundry bags
containing dresses, shirts, blouses, skirts, women's and
men's underwear, bed linen, and children's clothes onto the
floor of our tiny shack. We examined the clothes, especially
the women's undergarments, with great curiosity, and were
moved to disgust when we saw the stains and caught the
peculiar smell that seemed always to attach to white people's clothes.

One day, picking up a pair of striped silken bloomers
to scrutinize at leisure Ma-Mlambo laughed. "Oh God!
Mkulunkulu! A funny lot they are to wear such things!
Whoever heard of women putting on things like this. They
call them *amadilozi.* Drawers!" She chuckled, her mouth
twisted humorously. Traditional African women did not
wear pants and Ma-Mlambo and her cronies found these
sartorial odds and ends a subject of mirth. But mother was
not amused. Disapprovingly she snatched the garment from
Ma-Mlambo's hands. "Not in front of the child!" she said
righteously, noticing my interest.

Ma-Mlambo laughed even more heartily, "I agree.
These things are not fit for the eyes of a young man. Turn

your eyes aside, my child!" Saying this, she immediately howled, "And look at the stains!" Ma-Mlambo sat down on a low stool and watched my mother, elbow-deep in soap-suds, washing the dirt off our masters' clothes. Later the two gossiped in the front room while my mother laboriously pressed the clothes with an iron heated by charcoal.

Though my mother, Nonkanyezi, had struggled heroically against insuperable odds to live by a moral code she had brought with her from the countryside, the city was not to be withstood for long. The city was soon to change everything. It had changed many before her. It was soon to change my mother, too. It changed me certainly. At first nothing more than my mother's outward appearance seemed to have changed. After our arrival in the city, she had discarded her traditional dress of leather skirt and beads and in their place she now wore a variety of cheap Indian prints and would painfully wobble about in her newly acquired high-heel shoes. Later the change became more profound. The first signs of the greater upheaval to come was mother's conversion by an itinerant gospel preacher of the Church of Zion. A handsome, bearded fellow this preacher was, with the sharp piercing eyes of a zealous prophet. Soon our Saturday nights and Sunday mornings were ringing with the resounding noise of Zion-ists shouting praises to the Lord, speaking in tongues, and rocking to the accompaniment of a single drum.

The members of the Church of Zion wore long white flowing robes secured by green, blue, and red cords, which made them resemble the pictures of Christ's disciples we often saw in the illustrated Bible. The men wore their hair and beards long, for they were under injunction not to shave until Christ's second coming. Gabela exercised great authority, especially over the women members of the congregation. As the mesmeric leader with the hot piercing eyes, he seemed not only irresistible to women but was also apparently endowed with great healing powers. Formidable yet gentle, his hands were large, and he was known to have cured many hysterical women simply by laying his huge hands on their heads and shoulders—though some said his hands wandered to forbidden places—while calling upon the Lord to lift the heavy load from a sister's frail shoulders.

My mother's involvement with the Zionists mercifully lasted for only two years, after which an unfortunate incident with Gabela resulted in her leaving the Church altogether. She not only left the Church, but for the first time something was released within her that entirely transformed her character. I never found out the exact nature of her complaint against Gabela, but there was enough in her behavior to indicate that something had gone seriously amiss the day the prophet called at our house to lay hands on my mother, who was feeling slightly feverish with the inception of flu. The rupture, when it occurred, was to become permanent. The denouement to Gabela's career as a preacher and healer came a little later when, abandoning his flock to the wolves of other Zionist churches, he suddenly ran off with a deacon's young wife, taking with him all the congregation's funds from the bank. That was the last anybody ever heard of him or the deacon's wife. Whatever the nature of my mother's encounter with the prophet, its lasting and damaging effects on her personality were unmistakable. Her sentimental education was now apparently complete.

Never a cynic before, always fun-loving yet quietly modest, quick to perceive the passions she excited in men, but never so vain as to encourage them, eager, witty, yes, but always mindful of the Sibiya reputation of which she was now custodian in this intemperate city, she had seemed to many people the very model of what a self-respecting Zulu widow should be. But overnight, all that, her personality, her looks, her very soul, seemed to have been completely transformed. The men who had previously hovered around her like flies without daring to get any nearer—men who gazing with abject despondent lust at her incredible beauty had nonetheless treated her with grave if fretful respect—sensed the change immediately. In their attitude they now became more familiar, more intimate, even lewd. She did not seem to mind this; she even seemed to respond to their sexual entreaties.

Along with the rest of her personality my mother's body, too, seemed to have been transformed. In the countryside she had been very slim; she was now fuller, more buxom, more bright-eyed, invariably bubbling with vitality. It seemed that even if she had wanted to she could no longer hide her gaiety, which appeared now to be always about to spill over into a flare more dangerous than a dozen hells. She sang, she laughed, she danced like someone possessed. A current of ceaseless animation connected her to the jovial lust of men around her. Her toothy smiles, her dimpled copper-colored cheeks, her extravagantly hued skirts and brightly colored *doeks*, even her voice, which had always been so pure yet so close to hysteria, had become part of an arsenal she employed for the conquest of the world of city men, the tight-fisted world of money, of desperate township intrigues, and numerous petty struggles.

She had long ago stopped taking in washing, and to Ma-Mlambo's great satisfaction, in order to continue paying for my schooling, she had finally succumbed to the temptation of running a *shebeen*. Thus had my mother, like many of the women of Mkhumbane, finally ended as a seller of bootleg liquor. Many came to her shack to drink, many came to look for glamorous city women, but most came only to bask in the sunshine of my mother's charms and warm dimpled smiles and her dazzling good looks.

To me this was a source of great dissatisfaction, even bitterness. Although I recognized the pressures that had driven my mother to run a *shebeen* and, indeed, could not ignore the extent to which I benefited from the proceeds brought in by such an enterprise, I could no longer feel that my home was my own, what with the comings and goings at all hours of day or night: the noise, the drunkenness, the wanton frolics everywhere! The whole business was getting on my nerves. To study I had to take refuge in Ma-Mlambo's large, three-roomed shack, where the talkative but kindly old woman had set a room aside for my use.

Everywhere around the shacks, men called my mother's name, "Nonkanyezi! Nonkanyezi!" Already driven mad by *skokiaan* and the abandoned music of the new dance bands, their eyes hungry for my mother's hot mouth, for those lips that were always laughing, always painted, always promising more than they could rightly deliver, men buzzed like bees around a sweet-smelling but cankerous flower. Sometimes a strong man, with an uncommon personality, was permitted to dance with my mother, to the frustrated rage of the other drinkers. One such man

I remember clearly: big and strong, with red obsessive eyes. Over his mouth he had a dapper mustache and when he opened his mouth, flashing white teeth shone in it. He was called Big Joe and he was said to have come from what was then known as Nyasaland. Though this man laughed often, his laughter was internal; he seemed a man apart from others. His eyes appeared to mock at others' sexual frustrations. Always you had the feeling that he never tried with women. He just watched and waited. To the sexual blandishments of the women he responded with an easy smile, but he did nothing about it. He drove women mad. Big Joe was said to have killed another man once. A clever Jewish lawyer had gotten him off scot-free. Later, he had become a leader on the docks. He was always going to meetings. Men sought him out for counsel. Several times he led the workers out on strike for more pay, and there were battles with the police. It was obvious people respected Big Joe, but they never liked him. Many feared and envied him. One night, in a room behind the store room, I saw why. The big man, who had never even seemed to look at my mother before, this man whose studied indifference to my mother's most obvious provocations had excited surprised comment and speculation, was pressed hard against Nonkanyezi! My mother's clothes were in complete disarray, one naked breast had popped out of place, her brown shoulders gleamed like polished teak in the half-light, her entire body quivering in sensuous exhausted passion. She still tried in that moment of fateful fusion to struggle against Big Joe's wide encompassing arms, but obviously without much conviction. Big Joe's roving hand, tender yet strong, fumbled among tearing undergarments, fumbled, groped, rifled.

Big Joe and my mother were in shadow, their darker limbs laid bare, entwining, shining dimly under the unfathomable gaze of a starlit night. Like a dumb suffering beast, Nonkanyezi allowed herself to be pawed, and finally languished against the breast of the big man, a woman still haughty but humbled by a seemingly seething lust. Then all at once, as though a world had suddenly turned on its side, the man and the woman began to move together. In a steady, ever-increasing rhythm, they moved and moved and moved together while the world seemed to whirl around me like a gigantic spinning wheel.

Transfixed, not daring even to breathe, I watched them, astonished.

My mother Nonkanyezi had really changed.

15

These are digressions, I know. Hopeless detours. Evasions. At the beginning, I wanted to talk only of myself, of my own feelings, of my own attitudes. I wanted to put on record that I have learned a great deal in my twenty-five years of living. Though I did not graduate, I spent three years at the university before being kicked out for leading a protest strike against segregated classes. I know about a few things that great thinkers have pondered, I know what many poets and novelists have said. Was it not an eminent French poet, after all, who said, "We must get out of this century or have reason for staying in it!"? I have read. I have worked. I have worked at a succession of jobs. For a while I was timekeeper for a firm of building contractors. I have worked as a clerk for the Bantu administration. I've been an assistant in a big city bookshop. And I have lived, always, resentfully, on the fringes of a white world that tried to keep me out. But I'm different from my father. Thanks to my mother, that indefatigable "*Shebeen* Queen," I went to school, then to university, and I know what my father did not suspect: the white world that he hated and feared so much is built on so much shifting sands. It will not last. It will be swept away. That is what history teaches us. It is the history Professor Van Niekerk should have taught me, because it was getting to know that history, independently by private study and diligent reading, that saved me (you may smile at the irony) from a self-destructive rage. I became strong and defiant without real hatred in me.

Of course, there is an element of luck in all this. Luck. What a joke! A gallows bird talking of luck. Ah, but why mention my imminent execution? As the good Dr. Dufré always complains, I'm too morbid! I cannot stay away from the subject. Anyway, after my Senior Certificate, passed, as they say, with flying colors, the proud Lutheran Fathers who saw the pass list were only too happy to arrange a scholarship for me at the University of Natal. Suddenly the world all at once became for me both larger and narrower. Student life assumed its own rhythm of lectures, tutorials, protest meetings, demonstrations. For most classes, we black students were segregated, of course. We received our lectures in a barnlike lecture hall on the grounds of the Indian technical college. For a few courses, however, we were allowed to invade the sanctity of the "Whites Only" campus, where we shared classes with resentful white students.

Sometimes, asleep in my cell, I have nightmares in which I receive visits from old Professor Van Niekerk. His batlike face is wrapped up in cotton wool. He always arrives carrying an immense manuscript with pages from which words have been carefully erased. Laughing, he hands me this book and bids me to walk into the future by following the instructions inscribed in it. Van Niekerk, that ogre, that racist pig, that academic fraud! Yet outside these dreadful dreams, it must be said that the real Van Niekerk had a certain macabre charm. On the first day of term he said (almost invariably he addressed himself only) to the amazed white students, "Well! Well! Today, ladies and gentlemen, we have among us some rather unexpected visitors!" He gave only a weary smile, his brown-rat mustache quivering as though stirred by the smallest breeze. "These are the fortunate few students who have come from other national groups that make up the population of this our happy, sunny South Africa!" At this witticism he grinned greedily like a monkey discerning corn ripe enough for a bite. "Their presence among us, I am sure, will arouse in you different emotions and different sensations. Others among you may even see this as a small but significant drift toward eventual amalgamation of races."

Later I would notice that Van Niekerk almost never used the word "integration" if he could help it. It was as if this word alone carried within it the damning powers of the incubus. "This assumption, I dare say, is all too easy to make," Van Niekerk went on, "but I'm bound to say, so far as our non-white peoples are concerned, it is completely unwarranted. My experience, and I can speak here only from my own experience, is that the Bantu, the Indian, and the Kleurling have proved to be as anxious as we are to preserve their racial purity!" Even Van Niekerk did not seem to believe his own legend.

A blonde girl with green-blue eyes and a loose sexy mouth laughed uproariously at this, and Van Niekerk raised one surprised, questioning eye. The blonde instantly felt rebuked and shifted uneasily in her seat. "Excuse me, Professor Van Niekerk," she said defensively, responding to an unasked question, "but how do you know black people don't wish to 'amalgamate,' as you put it?" Other white faces of different shapes and sizes, crowned with gold, brown, or dark hair, all marked by various shades of astonishment at the girl's audacity, swiveled round to stare openmouthed at her. I must say this query should have alerted me once and for all to the fact that, given half a chance, white women will always cause trouble on race questions. Alas, I found that out only too late. Domus Maynard, the only colored student among us, spoke up at once. "Professor Van Niekerk, I am not sure that I understand you correctly, but many colored people like myself must wonder if they still possess any racial purity to defend after your people made sure to mingle with the blacks in order to produce us brown folk!"

In my dreams I can still see Van Niekerk's face in a state of complete shock as if he had been shown a ghost (of Christmas Past, perhaps). His white hair was standing on end. His long face, which is like the front of a horse, had turned red, then pale in quick succession. His pointed nose sniffed the air, one upturned eye staring at the ceiling and another rolling downward. His loose mouth drooled with a purposeless and undefined lust. An ugly face. After a while, he began again as though nothing had happened. He made some preliminary remarks about the subject of history he was going to teach, more relevantly about African history. His need to humble us black students was accentuated by every injury he felt to have sustained from Domus' words.

"A great historian who needs no introduction to some of us," Van Niekerk resumed, "once said of our beloved continent—and I think with a certain amount of justice—that before the white man came there was no African history to speak of in this darkest of the Dark Continents. Whether we like it or not, African history commences with the arrival on African soil of the first white man. The history of Africa is the history not of black Africans but of white men in a foreign environment. Ladies and gentlemen, I invite you for a minute to meditate on this inexpressible irony!"

Apart from the blonde with green-blue eyes who was surreptitiously painting her fingernails, the white students looked awed by the extent to which fate had thrust them into the unhappy role of bearing such a heavy burden. They became quiet and meditative, as Van Niekerk had urged them. Hosein, the Indian student who always sat on my left, began to giggle uncontrollably. The white students were outraged at the extent of his impudence. After all there were only five of us black students who had been allowed the rare privilege of attending Van Niekerk's select classes under the grand title "Themes of African History." The white students continued to see us as interlopers who should have shown proper gratitude. From different parts of the room there were hisses in an attempt to quiet Hosein, but the contrary appeared to be the effect of these disapproving noises. Hosein was unable to control his mirth. His giggles became guffaws and his guffaws became howls of ecstatic laughter. Soon the other black students were joining in, including myself, I regret to say.

Van Niekerk turned one eye upward and the other downward. "I'm surprised some of you find this situation sufficiently comical to arouse so much mirth." Gravely, disapprovingly, his face as red as a beet, Van Niekerk glared at us. His grin, when it came, was more ferocious than his grimace, his shiny white teeth were clenched tightly together in a threatening, tormented defensiveness. Finally he uttered his pronouncement: "I should not have thought," Van Niekerk shouted above sniggers, "that lack of historical enterprise in such a vast continent merited a response of such remarkable levity. Rather, I would have thought it should be cause for concern about the nature of what I regard as the great African tragedy in which we are all involved.

"Ladies and gentlemen," Van Niekerk went on remorselessly, "we only have to look to the north of us to see what is happening. The fact that we live in a continent marked by the absence of human thought, science, and philosophy, a continent in which there is a visible lack of art, music, and architecture, is not one that we can regard as an occasion for humor. For is it not one of the appalling facts of our circumstance that in Africa we are surrounded not by monuments to the human spirit and human achievement, but by a startling absence, an oppressive spiritual vacuum, an imponderable silence?"

This was it! The final word! At last, exhausted by his own eloquence, Van Niekerk staggered back from the podium, mopping his brow with a soiled white handkerchief. Several heads amongst white students were brought together in various corners of the room. A buzz of subdued admiration flowed like an underground stream. By this time Hosein was rolling in his chair, he was laughing so much that tears were streaming down his cheeks. Then, as suddenly as if someone had administered a dose of a sleep-inducing drug, Hosein promptly fell asleep in his chair, his head rolling backward, his mouth open, a rare beatific smile still lingering on his face, while Van Niekerk, more astonished than outraged, leaned forward to observe this new phenomenon.

16

At the beginning of my third year at the university, there was a series of strikes and demonstrations, all of which were designed to promote a campaign against racial discrimination. A few white students and professors, usually of liberal or left-wing persuasion, joined us. Climaxing one such strike, a sit-in was called to occupy the principal's office, a sit-in that became rather boisterous (a few flowerpots were broken, someone had watered the rest with urine) and that was quelled only with the aid of riot police. As a result, some students were severely beaten up and had to be hospitalized. I was lucky to escape with only a fractured arm.

How I got involved as a key figure in all these battles is not clear even to me. At first I had done no more than speak at union meetings in support of various resolutions passed to put on record our increasing frustrations with the university senate. Later, though I made great effort to shun the limelight, I found myself drawn more and more into the web of politics. I was being elected to more and more committees, entrusted with the task of holding consultations with the authorities. I was instructed to protest against this or that injustice. As a frequent member of these delegations, my name came to be well known. Several times I was interviewed by the newspapers, which meant in time I would be interviewed by the police. Finally, I received from the senate a strongly worded letter warning of possible expulsion if I persisted with my disruptive activities. I did not take these threats very seriously, but the inevitable happened after May Day, when demonstrations called in support of a student demand for the removal of Professor Van Niekerk from our racially mixed classes in view of his provocative behavior again ended in a series of clashes with the police. A few windows in Warwick Avenue were broken by well-aimed rocks. As one who had been warned repeatedly by the governing body, I was summarily expelled. Thus came to an end my career as a student of the University of Natal.

17

Sometimes when the mood takes him, Dufré discourses to me on the subject of love. Perhaps as a result of contemplating my own predicament too long, or perhaps because of his own personal experiences in the past, Dufré tends to take an unreasonably pessimistic view of the subject. He calls the necessity to love another human being "in an individualized sense" an unmitigated tragedy. "Certainly not a gift from the gods as some like to think," Dufré says darkly, his eyes flashing behind his glasses.

"When it is urgent and demanding, love is both a

threat and an impossible prison," Dufré asserts. "It has nothing to do with what Americans like to sing about in their popular music—moonlight in Vermont and stars over Alabama. On the contrary, love is hot, dark, and dangerous, and mostly has to do with failure, loss, and running away, with betrayal and treachery. Even cruelty is part of it."

This is the only time since I have known him that Dufré uses language as if it were meant to convey some meaning, something precious and truthful without which we would all be poorer. It is the only time, too, that I have detected in him hidden springs of emotion. No longer just the scientist, calm, inquiring, and disinterested, he is a man like all of us, struggling with the unknown mysteries of the human heart. The language shows it.

Dufré's passionate address on the subject of love on an unusually gray morning with a sky like lead overhead reminds me of many things I would prefer to forget. One: at school I remember a pretty young girl my own age who had always looked at me with something like shock and surprise. A girl with very deep black eyes and very black velvet skin, delicate and nervous, also incurably shy and frightened. She never spoke to me nor to anyone else about what was in her heart. Then one day something snapped and she gave me a resounding slap, which took me wholly by surprise. We had been playing at something or other, and I asked her why she had done it. She trembled violently and then broke into tears.

"Because I love you and I hate you and I do not know what to do!" At the time I was only shocked, but I understood nothing from the incident. Her tantrum had merely puzzled me. Today, I understand a little of what that girl felt. I understand, too, Veronica Slater's alternating boldness and fear, her craving and revulsion, her complicity and her final turning against me. It was part of the same obsession, part of the same audacity, part of the same shame. I also understand something of my own fascination with the girl, my wholly inappropriate desire for a white woman in a country, as Dufré never tires of reminding me, which loses no time in hanging black boys who poach in hunting grounds reserved for whites only. But so many things were involved in my own choice of arena for rebelling against the narrow straitjacket in which society was determined to imprison me. Lust was one of them, I admit, but why lust for a white woman? There were plenty of black girls on whom I could have vented my lust—if lust and nothing but lust was what I suffered from. May it not have had something to do with my expulsion from the university, my loss of anchorage or sense of direction, my final despair? At any rate, my passion grew out of humble beginnings, a game that both Veronica and I played with elaborate observance of the rules.

Finally she won, of course. Yes, Veronica is the only one who came out of this gigantic scandal a clear winner. Perhaps this was unavoidable considering how loaded the dice were against me from the beginning. All the same, both the girl and I tried to maintain a minimum of decorum required of those who, living in a country that sternly forbids racial mixing, still feel compelled to graze over on the other side of the fence. Part of the unstated rules of the game, enforced by nothing less than fear of imprisonment that would follow discovery, was the preserving, day after day, week after week, of this harrowing torment of anonymity.

From the very beginning, Veronica and I were deprived of what lovers the world over are permitted to enjoy at the burgeoning of an affair. We could not indulge in an exchange of names or even enjoy the lighthearted banter of a budding friendship. We could not part with a few well-chosen compliments or make an odd suggestive remark about clothes, looks, feelings, emotions, hungers, and longings. We could trade no compliments, which, in the normal course of events, make up the unchanging ritual of courtship. Right up to the climax of this affair, which was the union of two bodies, we were technically strangers to each other. Veronica and I could use no words beyond the primitive language of looks and gestures, beyond the surreptitious grunts and murmurs when desire became too insupportable. In short, we could not declare ourselves.

Since we were lovers in everything but name, sometimes the suffering showed: in the ravenously hungry stares we directed at each other, in the suppressed tension behind the hooded eyelids, in the subtle droop at the corners of the mouth, or even in the momentary trembling of the lips when, unexpectedly, we came across each other in the streets. I say all this purely out of my own observation of the girl, of course. I cannot say what my own face showed, though I should think quite as much, if not more.

Once, when leaving the beach by separate routes, the English girl and I collided at the entrance of the small tobacco shop at the end of the esplanade. We were both so overcome by the shock of this unexpected encounter, occurring as it did far from our usual "trysting" place on the often deserted spot on the beach, that we both behaved exactly like two clumsy lovers who, meeting each other by chance, find themselves at a loss for the right kind of words to utter. So clumsy and bashful, in fact, were we that I am surprised the other white people who must have witnessed the incident failed to notice anything odd in our behavior. Anyone but white South Africans, a people so accustomed to regarding the blacks as nothing but pegs on which to hang their hats, would have surely remarked that something was amiss here. They would have been forced to detect in our shy and clumsy behavior—in the startled expressions and tentative guilty smiles on our faces, in the eyes quickly averted but not so quickly as to conceal the very obvious fact of mutual recognition—I repeat, anyone would have seen in these odd gestures not the reaction of an innocent white woman bumping into a clumsy black man; they would have seen not the harmless collision between a white madam, both irreproachable and unapproachable, and a native male, timid and helplessly immobilized by fear, fear of that contact with a woman of a "superior race," which we are all supposed to have. They would have seen in the girl's blushes, in her shifting guilty eyes veiled by long fluttering eyelashes, in her wide distorted mouth from whose trembling lips a sound like a wordless murmur seemed to struggle for utterance, a surprised embarrassed meeting of lovers who were visibly vexed by the necessity to conceal their knowledge of each other from the world. They would have needed fewer signs to alert them to this fact than what the girl and I had already offered. Supposedly strangers to each other, yet so manifestly familiar with each other's faces, at the very least, we declared our mutual guilt the moment we bumped into each other. The strain, the nervous agitation, was immense, for not only did we come face to face for the first time at that tobacconist shop, but we touched flesh to flesh.

There were a few white people around as I remember: an old man inspecting a set of briar pipes, a flabby middle-aged blonde woman gazing myopically at some holiday postcards, two young girls in swimsuits exchanging harmless sexual innuendos with the gray-faced tobacconist behind the counter. At one corner of the shop, still clutching recently bought packets of cigarettes, two big-shouldered, red-faced Springbok types were arguing about the respective merits of two Rugby players. A lingering fragrance of tobacco, suntan oil, and wet skin recently emerged from the sea pervaded the tiny shop. After buying my own packet of cigarettes as self-effacingly as possible, I walked toward the door only to bump into Veronica Slater, who had already changed into smart street clothes. She chose that moment to step into the shop, perhaps to buy the very same brand of cigarettes I had just purchased, such being the vagaries of fate. Suddenly, the very air, which until then had seemed entombed in a tunnel of a warm lethargic afternoon, became light as motes. Veronica and I did not so much as run into each other as *crush* into each other's bodies, falling about each other into what was almost an accidental embrace. Still damp from suntan oil and swimming, Veronica bumped into me with the force of a clumsy young elephant, her full breasts charging ahead of her. To this day I remember exactly the feeling, the prickly sensation of my skin as our bodies touched, caressed. I can hear the singing of blood in my veins at the feel of the silk of the garment she wore, the smooth texture of the skin on her naked arms.

At the instance of our collision, something fell from her hand. A comb? A hat? A handbag? I cannot remember. I spoke then, "I'm so sorry! Please, excuse me!" And bent down to pick up whatever had fallen from her hand. "No, no! It's entirely my fault!" She spoke in a lowered tone at once courteous and surprisingly shy for a white woman addressing a native. Heard for the first time, the sound of her voice was startlingly mellifluous, not at all shrill, whining or high-pitched as were most white South African voices I had heard. It was low, tranquil, and musically modulated like the sigh of the sea at night. Whether from embarrassment at so accidental an encounter or perhaps simply from her eagerness to retrieve her property, not knowing exactly what she was doing, Veronica had gone down on her knees at the very moment that I bent down to pick up her article so that the two of us, crouching together, had our faces nearly touching. Our heads were lowered together at the exact moment, and her still-damp hair brushed quickly against my face while her wide sensual mouth hovered handsomely close to mine. Feeling rather foolish, but excited by such proximity, we both hesitated just an instant. She raised her eyes level to mine, and staring into those very deep-green pupils, where light and darkness seemed to blend so unnaturally, I felt as though I had plunged naked into a disturbed pool of water. In her agitation, I was aware of her intense stillness. The color in the curve of her cheeks became very vivid. But though obviously as agitated as I was, Veronica could not refrain from flashing a provokingly mocking smile, so familiar to me from our many meetings on the beach, as slow and hesitant yet shiningly joyful and carnal. It had the power to revive every thread of desire she had long ago woven around my enchanted heart.

All this happened in only a matter of seconds, then we were rising together and I saw in that instant the full white throat above the low-cut dress, the high magnificent breasts beneath the flimsy cloth begin to heave and throb like the swell of a large ocean wave. It was a single moment, but all the same, a moment charged with such torment of spirit, hinting at all those undivulged secrets of the heart we had thought we were so adept at concealing.

There was also delight in that encounter. Before I had straightened up, I had not only caught a whiff of the suntan oil she used on her skin, the strong, not very subtle perfume beneath the oil, but I had also acquired a firm conviction that this was the start of something neither of us could modify or control very easily. What this was, I didn't know. How it was to end, I didn't know, either. Had we been in any country other than South Africa, I would have seen it as a happy omen, perhaps the likely beginning of an affair. As it was, I regarded this encounter with a certain amount of foreboding. After all, however accidental and tantalizingly brief, this was the first physical contact I had had with the English girl. From then on, she was no longer to be simply a dream, a phantom, a ghost, a mirage created by my own bedazzled eyes out of the hot sands of the beach. I had felt her breast crushed against my breast. I had felt the brush of her hair against my face. And the girl, tremulous and gleaming with her invincible color and excitement, had smiled into my face. Those huge green eyes, so modestly sheltered behind flickering eyelids, had seemed in that single moment of contact to pose a question for which I had no answer. "Entirely my fault!" she had said. "It's entirely my fault!" Whatever else followed would be her fault. This she had acknowledged.

18

That night there was the smell of rain, I remember, on the overheated pavements, a suppressed murmur in the garden foliage behind Ma-Mlambo's shack, and I went to bed smelling heat and listening to the silent stir in the leaves. When sleep came, it was an uneasy, troubled sleep during which I was haunted by white, harrowing dreams. One of those dreams survives in my memory with sufficient clarity. The rest dissolve into fragments, into incoherent images and fleeting impressions, black shapes and phantoms behind which, I'm sure, hide my innermost fears, behind which burn all those denied secret wishes and the gnawing private guilts.

From a jumble of memory I recall only wanton ogres and fanciful dervishes executing their fiendish spectral dances in that vast deep of my innermost consciousness. Try as I may to conjure up these shapes into some kind of coherent order, to construct out of the chaotic jumble of images some meaning, in the end I find nothing but shadows. Everything dissolves finally into a miasma of guilt and shame, and something more perplexing—fear! It is as though the mere recall of the outline of a dream will bring its own retribution.

Nevertheless, the vague shape of that dream remains in my mind to this day like a searing wound, like a memory of an exquisite torture undergone a long time ago but whose recollection it is hard to erase. The locale is blurred but the atmosphere is that of a Zulu court. A gaudy Zulu monarch sits in judgment over me surrounded by his *indunas* and other courtiers. What crime I have committed it is impossible to say. I seem to be standing on a pedestal before a huge assemblage of courtiers and armed guards and I am naked to my toes. It seems I have stood there all day long. I feel so tired. My legs are almost sagging under my body, but I manage to support my weight very well because all the time I can see the chieftain on his throne glaring at me with his flaming red eyes.

Abruptly, a most amazing sight presents itself before my eyes and a shiver goes through me like cold steel glancing through naked flesh. A moment longer and I feel as though my body has been warmed by an invisible fire or touched by a million hot hands, for there in front of me stands the king's daughter, the most beautiful girl I have ever seen and she is wearing nothing but her beads, as they say, and a sort of shimmering blue veil wrapped around her beautiful limbs. Tall, regal, smooth-limbed, with high breasts like pillars of brown salt and eyes as cold as a serpent's, she walks into the arena with her lithe swaying step, a smile on her mouth that is as provocative as it is noncommittal.

The girl begins to dance for me and everybody watches to see how much I will be able to stand of her calculated provocation. This is my test. I have been warned: at the very first sign of physical lust my head will go to the chopping block. I am meant to hold firm, to resist all desire, to hold firm on my flesh, in short to prove my ability to overcome temptation, which is the basis of all wicked deeds and earthly sorrow. But what can a man do? As the girl continues her provocative dance, it seems as though I were standing alone upon a high mountain where an icy wind cannot cool my hot feverish brow. The veins in my head throb like piston engines and I can feel my blood travel from my heart to my head, warm, quick, then back to my belly, my thighs, and legs. There is a soft stirring inside my legs threatening me with disaster.

I must try and hold on, I tell myself. It is the only chance I have to escape my terrible fate, the chance I have to stay alive. Try and think of something else to take your thoughts off this incredible scene!

But now, like a well-trained stripper doing the Dance of the Seven Veils, the king's daughter—my temptress—has begun to remove her transparent veil, disclosing a wealth of physical beauty extraordinary to behold. Frightened, I cannot bear to watch, but I also cannot bear not to watch. I stand as though mesmerized by her trembling high breasts and the shimmering young buttocks, by the hands as they casually brush slowly and delicately up and down her glossy, brown thighs, moving maddeningly up to the reddish black crown of her feathered glory. My head begins to get dizzy. My heart pounds like a chain-gang hammer. A slow fire descends to my loins. Beads of sweat break from my brow. She is dancing too close to me, her body almost brushing against mine, turning round and round my limbs. Driven to an almost manic frenzy by the girl's sexual taunts, I feel myself losing control. Oh, God, help me! I can't hold out! Oh, ancestors, fathers of my fathers, help me! But no, there is no help. From now on it appears I can only let myself go. It is a moment of supreme relief, that total surrender to an impulse older than human law, more ancient than civilization itself, for it is only by penetrating into the forbidden portals of that royal hearth that I feel I can achieve total liberation, then die.

I remember thinking at the time that if this were the way to die, what a wonderful way to go! But just as I was about to shoot the princess full of white birds, I saw the king rise from his throne, his face terrible to behold. A murmur like a high wind on a distant plain arose from the assembled crowd. He was moaning deep in his throat and in a voice full of unspeakable anguish he cried out furiously, "Seize the traitor! Seize and kill him instantly!" But it was too late for me to stop. I felt my body burst through the inner sanctum of that royal hearth, and once I was joined to the princess, I was simply indifferent to my fate. A soldier approached with a glittering spear and at once raised it to pierce me through the heart, a single thrust, which instantly severed me from the source of my greatest delight and transport.

"Obviously a wish-fulfillment dream," Dufré said excitedly when I told him about it. "What is very surprising," he added, reflectively, "is that the dream material should have been so obvious in their postulates, their enactment of ambition for sexual gratification. No attempts whatsoever at symbolism. No mushrooms. No climbing of trees or pressing through dark tunnels." He shook his head. "You know, of course, who is represented by your terrible autocratic king?"

"King Cetshwayo!" I said, laughing. "No, Shaka or perhaps King Bekuzulu!"

"Mr. Sibiya." The Swiss doctor sighed wearily. "Please, be serious."

19

It is possible, as Dufré suggested, that this dream was about the white girl. I don't know. I don't care. I know only that as soon as morning came, I was up and ready to leave for the city, ready to drop like a stricken bird on that isolated part of the beach where I was wont to keep vigil for Veronica Slater, my serene temptress, my tormentor. Nothing, it seemed, could detain me much longer in Cato Manor. A heart in love is a heart in flight, the body simply follows where passion leads, and a doomed passion is the most dangerous because it is the most powerful of all.

As far as my mother was concerned, I suppose I was like any other unemployed youth, daily rushing into the city's center to join queues at the Labor Bureau in the hope of being hired. Little did she suspect that I spent these precious hours of the day at the beach, my blood seething, fighting the heat, the dust, the flies, hunger, heedless of discomfort, for the sake of a glimpse of a girl who displayed as much concern for my helplessly distracted adoration as the most exalted queen might show for the demented love of one of her humblest subjects.

But what did I care? What did I care for the anguished hours of waiting in the moist heat, hours of waiting in the poisoned, sulphurous air, suffering in the languor of insensate afternoons, which seemed to disseminate nothing but death? At the sight of that face surrounded by a mop of surging auburn hair, at the look of inexpressible sorrow around that droopingly sensual mouth, I was transported to new regions of heavenly bliss. For the sake of that temporary bliss, I was prepared to endure discomfort: the morning rush hour on the buses, being jostled and pummeled by arms and elbows of passengers who, admittedly, had more pressing reasons to get to the city on time. I, on the contrary, was only following an obsession. But does love or even a blind obsession require sound reason or justification? All the way to town I listened with stupefied lack of comprehension to the continual din of passengers exchanging gossip, at the telling of jokes, witticisms, confidences. I sat immobile like a madman in one of those occasional fits of hypnotic paralysis when something seems to have been arrested at the core of their being. The noise went on unabating around me.

Among my people, going to work on a bus is an experience, an adventure. As in many other places where people without a parliament come to be thrown together, during its thirty minutes' run to town the bus becomes a great forum for the airing of political views, the expression of discontent, or the dispersal of useful information. Without wishing to hear you learn who has gone to jail, who has come out of it, who has run off with which businessman's wife, where the next police raids are expected, which politician is selling out to which city councilor. Every morning it is the same: gossip, anecdotes, the exchange of information or helpful expertise passed on with a kind of oiled-tongue fluency run rampant.

When the bus finally pulled up at the Durban Bus Station, there was the usual squad of iron-faced police waiting to check the identity documents of alighting passengers—passengers whose passes were not in order, passengers whose permits to live in the city had expired, those without any visible means of employment. In short, myself and thousands of others like myself, who lived a life of enforced idleness and criminality. However, that morning, balancing my needs to see the girl against the less pleasant prospect of spending a day or two in the clutches of the police, I was determined not to be caught in the net. As soon as I reached the exit door of the bus my body became transformed into a crumpled, twisted, crippled wreck of smashed-up limbs shuffling past the waiting police, walking sideways like a crab, shaky, trembling, drooling saliva, determined to drive the point home to my masters regarding my physical incapacity to do any kind of work, in fact, my utter uselessness as a possible prisoner.

To make myself even more obnoxious, I stretched forth my hand for a few coppers as I walked past in the extravagant gesture of a mendicant to whom the police were no object of terror. "A penny, my baas! Penny my baas!" I cried, thrusting my hand under their disapproving faces. In disgust, they waved me by. *"Gaan, jou bliksem!* Go on! Get out of here, you twisted carcass of stinking rubbish!" *"Dankie, my baas!"* I walked past. In a delicate limp, mumbling under my breath, "For the love of God, *my baas! My Kroon!"* Not until I was well out of sight did I straighten up and adjust my walk to its normal gait. Even then I did not relax my vigilance. All the time I was on the lookout for the police who lurked in every nook of the city, ready to pounce on unemployed blacks. Only when I reached the beach, with its pure white sands, its seawater glittering like scattered pearls under a wide curving sky, did I feel safe enough from the long arm of the law.

I have to explain that the beach is not beyond the reach of the flying squad, but the presence of so many white citizens, white people who may have been perfectly happy to vote for laws of harassment against blacks but who having voted have no stomach for witnessing the manner in which these laws are carried out, has an inhibiting effect upon the police. Beatings, torture are all right, necessary, even inevitable, but every one understands that such cruelty must be inflicted on the victim out of sight of the public gaze, especially out of the sight of the hordes of foreign tourists, who, chancing to witness such arrests and beatings, may carry away with them a less than cheerful picture of our sunny South Africa.

Having reached my usual spot on the beach, I at once threw myself gratefully upon the white sands and with a thumping heart awaited the arrival of Veronica, my secret paramour.

In the past, I had sometimes waited for an hour or more before the slim figure of the girl would make its appearance over the horizon, her brown hair lifting a bit in the breeze. Sometimes she would appear suddenly behind me, walking hesitantly past my prostrate body to cross the small stream that divided her side of the beach from mine. She would walk so close to where I lay on the sand I could see the fine pores of her skin on her shaved, gliding legs, smooth like polished wood. I could even sniff the gusts of perfume emanating from her body as it sauntered past me, leaving behind a rumor of fragrances as penetrating as the exhalations of a mountain rose. She would walk so close that had I reached out my hand, I could have touched her, but not once did either of us ever depart from the unstated policy of our silent compact not to speak. So near yet so far, for all the proximity we shared we might as well have been in different parts of the universe. We could feast our eyes upon each other's bodies but we could say nothing to each other to express what we felt. Words were dangerous; once spoken, they could never be unspoken. Harm, if it turned out that harm was the result, could never be undone. The girl understood this as much as I did. She understood that so far as the law was concerned, it was enough for people of the two races to "conspire" to break the Immorality Act for the courts to convict, even if the couple had not actually committed the sexual act itself. This knowledge, I believe, encouraged in both of us a certain amount of prudence and caution.

Sometimes waiting for Veronica to arrive, waiting for the ritual of uneasy, silent flirtation to begin, I would get drowsy and fall asleep. When I woke up, she would be already there, stretched out on the towel, her head cradled in her brown arms, watching me with eyes gleaming with annoyance at my inattentiveness, as if my momentary dozing showed lack of discipline or fidelity. Yet she was not alone in experiencing these periodic fits of resentment. I, too, was quick to succumb to feelings of pique at any imagined want of duty on her part. Once or twice, when she had failed to keep our silent rendezvous, the shock of disappointment I felt had been startling even to myself. A feeling of injury, of having been betrayed, of being stood up, would last all day and all night until the next time I saw her approach the beach with that careless stride of a child kicking pebbles. Just how clearly she understood how much I had missed her was obvious the moment she looked at me with that shifting guilty expression of eyes that seemed to make a plea for forgiveness. At the beginning, she would pretend indifference. She smoked. She read her cheap novels with the garish covers, but whenever our eyes happened to meet it was obvious even to her that I was sulking, that I wished her to know it, and she would raise her eyebrows questioningly. But she was also quite evidently a girl with a sly sense of humor. The hint of a smile around her drooping mouth indicated, if any further indication were needed, how keenly she was aware of the suffering her absence had caused. At such times, slowly changing her position on the towel, she would give me more than an ample view of her luxurious breasts, a view so deliberately prolonged that I had enough time to note the blue veins that ran down to the tip of her nipples, like an ore of a Kimberley mine.

That morning, waiting for Veronica to arrive, I lay on the white sands of the beach, unseeing like a tormented beast. The sun, which had lain hidden behind a dark cloud, had suddenly emerged to consume everything beneath it in a slow burning heat like the outbreak of a dreadful voluptuous fever. An hour passed. Another hour and still there was no sign of the girl. From a sea that sparkled like a cluster of jewelry under a thin paper sky, the sun was climbing slowly to its zenith. The smallest breeze stirred the fronds of the palm trees, and the sea smelled of salt and seaweed, an unfamiliar, unintelligible stillness interrupted only by the soft lapping sound of water exhausting itself against the jutting rocks, resting over everything as though a stupendous energy was seething underneath but in check. I could hear the rapid beating of my own heart as I lay on the sand waiting like a beast at bay crouching behind the tall wild grass. However, as the hours passed and the unbroken tension of a long wait began to press heavily upon my nerves, I was overcome by a new kind of terror and despair. Suppose she did not come? How to pass the day? How to sleep at night? Anxiety gripped my yearning heart like a vice, but for a while longer I endeavored to remain calm.

The big clock at the end of the esplanade suddenly struck twelve. I dozed. Woke up. Dozed. When I woke up, it was one o'clock and still there was no sign of Veronica anywhere. I thought with despair, remembering the awkward meeting at the tobacconist shop, its suddenness, perhaps also its unexpectedness, she will not come! She has taken fright! The crowds of bathers were beginning to leave for the seafront hotels and restaurants, followed in their wake by black boys who methodically combed the sands for abandoned watches or forgotten jewelry. From where I sat, huddled up, my arms wrapped around my knees, I watched a lone speedboat going by, slicing the water and raising a rush of spray. A saltless breeze was rising above the slow, drowsy afternoon heat like a somnolent alley cat prowling after an inattentive bird. When the clock struck three and there was no sign of the girl, I knew then Veronica would not come that day, and realizing this, a feeling of great desolation came over me as if a door had shut suddenly in my face, a feeling of such emptiness, such anguish and loneliness, that the very sky seemed to turn dark above the horizon of swirling, undulating waves. In front of my very eyes, as if an invisible hand were stirring up the salty wastes, the sea suddenly became very agitated. Waves as big as the mountains came crashing into shore. From the docks the horn of a loading vessel honked repeatedly, adding its fretful lamentation to the plaintive sounds of the late afternoon. With a sudden, bold decisiveness, I plucked myself up from the sands and without any clear notion of where I was headed, I found myself walking rapidly in the direction of the airport, traversing a wasteland of sand, rock, and heaps of industrial rubble, walking across an empty space in the direction, as I now realized, of the lone green-paned bungalow that stood discreet and isolated among a clump of trees and undergrowth. If nothing else, I had to catch a glimpse of the English girl.

···

20

"And how long did you remain then like a condemned man waiting for absolution outside that bungalow?" Dufré asked, watching my hands nervously playing with the ends of my prison uniform. My recollection of the girl, the fat man who appeared at the door with her, a cigar hanging loosely from gross, fleshy lips, was as vivid as if I were seeing them that very instant. The moment Veronica came down the wooden steps, followed by that fat white man, and saw me leaning against the apple tree just outside her gate, she stifled a cry of surprise, but too late. The man followed her gaze, saw me standing there, and frowned suspiciously. I heard him say, "What does the kaffir want? Do you know him?" And Veronica lied. "Some vagrant native, I suppose. How am I to know every stray native?" It was my turn to smile my bitterness. I saw the white man hesitate. "Everything properly locked up?" He had a thick foreign accent, like a Greek or a Lebanese. "Oh, come on, Sid!" Veronica said, coloring. "You know I have nothing of value to steal." They had reached the gate. Veronica turned to stare briefly at me, questioningly, before averting her gaze. Following her stare, the fat man looked hostile. He shouted, "What do you want?" I stopped leaning against the tree. "Nothing, baas." "Well go away from here. The missus doesn't want you hanging around here. You hear? Go away or I'll call the police."

"Sid, come on, we're late. He's broken no law," Veronica said impatiently. Again she turned to look at me quickly with those green eyes of hers, which were constantly opening and shutting in the light so that at times they looked violet, like pure sunset. Saying this, she started to walk away, followed reluctantly by the fat man who kept glancing behind to make sure I was following. On the esplanade I saw them getting into a snazzy white Porsche, which started at top speed in the direction of the docks. "And you saw this as an opportunity to break into a white woman's bungalow?" Dufré put in. "Surely this was lunacy on your part!"

"Perhaps. I don't know. I wasn't myself that day. I had never seen her with a man before! I suppose the shock was too great for me. Like discovering your best girl is secretly seeing another man."

"Ah, you were jealous?" Dufré breathed, almost a sigh. "Had it never occurred to you that you were nothing to this girl but a shadow with which she amused herself? That she had her own life to live? What's more, that in all fairness she was entitled to a little privacy?"

"To tell the truth, by then we were like lovers. I felt, perhaps unjustly, that I had claims upon her as strong as, if not stronger than, those of any other man."

Dufré nodded. "In short, you had become mad! Unhinged!"

"I suppose so."

"Go on. So you entered the bungalow. What did you see?"

"Nothing. An ordinary room sparsely furnished with a bed, a chest of drawers, a wardrobe, a wooden chest. A single shelf lined with books, a few unimportant pictures. An airy room. I liked it instantly. There was a certain unassuming openness about it that was very welcoming. But the single dominating feature of that room was the wide, high bed with its unembroidered white quilts and a pile of soft pillows, a comfortable bed with a suggestion of sovereign calm and purity of taste that surprised me. A spinster's room in a way. There was no suggestion of disorder. No suggestion that she and the fat man had made love. Naturally, I was apprehensive in case someone had seen me breaking in, so I did not linger too long in that room. I passed through a small door into the kitchen, where I noticed without too much interest the shiny pots and pans gleaming against the wall, and, without stopping, walked past, into the bathroom."

Dufré waited, the only sign of impatience the regular nervous drumming of his fingers upon the arm of his chair.

I was no longer conscious of his existence. Once again, I was standing in Veronica's bathroom, that palace of white marble, full of mirrors as if each one was there to reflect an aspect of her personality, to confirm her existence. I was standing in the middle of that bathroom, the most private area of her private life, feeling both bonded and free, conscious also of a horrible kind of duality within me, a perception of the fathomless depths of my desire. My head was swimming. I was dizzy. To break through this state of heightened consciousness I had to reacquaint myself with the physical world around me—the sensuous feel of cement slab beneath my feet, the soft white rug, the bright whitewash look of the bathroom walls.

Then it seemed as if my vision was failing. The bathroom walls began to wobble, to undergo a change under my very eyes; they assumed the aspect of a dreary whitewashed prison. A peculiar trick of my eyesight! Perhaps. In order to get a grip on myself, I concentrated my eyes on the toilet objects, trying to keep them apart in my mind. For what seemed to be a long time, I gazed at Veronica's clothes: at the nylon slips in shaded pinks, blues, and greens, and the scanty, elaborately embroidered bras, the nylon stockings dangling out of the laundry basket, and the lace panties hung like a conqueror's flags on the rail above the shower tap. On the rim of the sink there was a cluster of toothbrushes, eyebrow pencils, bottles of perfume, powder puffs, and lipsticks. So strong, in fact, was the impression these objects created of the occupier of the bungalow that they succeeded in taking my mind completely off my own sorry struggle with the nature of my hallucinations.

When I finally turned around, I caught a glimpse of my

face in one of the mirrors. I stared at my image with surprise as though a stranger's face were reflected there: the face was sharp, bony in fact, a smooth clean-shaven chin set squarely on a firm neck; and the mouth, somewhat loose and effeminate, had enough of the Sibiya squareness to give the face a look of an aggressive masculinity. My brow was my father's—heavy, somber, and smooth with a hairline starting back near the crown of my head. It was the black luster of the eyes that surprised me. They were so limpid that for a moment I had the illusion I was staring into someone else's eyes! It was while I stood there arrested by my own image in the mirror that I heard voices. A dog barked. Someone shouted, "Madelaine!" It was a man's voice, harsh, tired, impatient. Listening with a shortened breath, I heard from the back of the bungalow footsteps making a soft crunching sound on the gravel path. A woman's voice said, "Shall we go in and see if she is in?" The same male voice said brusquely, "What for? She's told us all we need to know about the property." The rest was lost in a confusion of voices speaking simultaneously, punctuated by the noise of a barking dog. I waited anxiously until the voices had faded away into the distance before I started to move rapidly toward the front door.

21

For the next three days I did not go to the beach. I was determined to break the habit of dependence, once and for all, and it was clear to me that my interest in the girl was no longer a simple matter of curiosity, a kind of game in which the girl and I were harmlessly engaged. Instead, it had assumed a form of necessity, threatening to undermine my mental stability. Breaking into the girl's flat, which could have led to my immediate arrest, was the culmination of a process: lack of any sense of direction, listlessness, inability to concentrate, daydreaming. I could no longer remember when last I had had a regular meal.

Before coming across the girl on the beach, reading, directed toward no particular purpose save the delectation of the mind, had been one of my greatest delights. Now, if I took up a book, I could hardly make any sense of it. My mind wandered, and between myself and the personages who peopled the novels I read interposed, uninvited, the lewd, mocking figure of the girl on the beach, turning over and over on her spread-out towel or rug. In my mind's eye I could see her lambent breasts flashing like white beacons behind her protective arms. I couldn't drive her out of my mind.

Nighttime was the worst time of all. Sometimes to relieve my jangling nerves I roamed the township's streets, past the bus depot with market-stall women selling fatcakes by candlelight, past the Indian stores on whose shop fronts the young *tsotsis* hung about like clusters of motionless flies, the street with its lights, people and movement forming a single chain of aimless activity—people everywhere with a great deal of time on their hands and no idea of what to do with it. The dark areas of Cato Manor were a little sad now with an emptiness, shadowy and sinister. Yet despite the sordid meretriciousness of the neighborhood, there was a great supportive energy to the way the sweaty streets felt, the people dawdling on the pavements, the children scampering behind the gray iron shacks, the old men and women shuffling belatedly into front rooms, pausing to peer with incredulous wonder at the bright carnival of summer being endlessly enacted in the streets. I watched the keen, knife-blade boys with their arms around the pliant waists of languid girls, and middle-aged women who stared out of open windows, their rounded breasts tilting out of flimsy summer dresses. All this throbbing life was somehow good and marvelous, and the goodness in the streets was matched only by the goodness of the sky, which hung low, scorching everything to a bawdy neon-lit pink. Indeed, the whole soporific atmosphere of summer had deepened suddenly into something festive and elemental—a deathless pagan energy wide with the flesh and movement, which was possibly the reason my heart ached so much with this absurd longing to see the English girl again.

It was the end of the third day of my "fast" and already I knew my resistance had been in vain. The following day I would go to the seaside once again and would haunt the neighborhood of that green-painted wooden bungalow until I saw the girl emerge or go in; my resistance, such as it was, was at an end. Away from the seaside, from the girl, that is, I felt only more acutely the lack of my own sense of worth and direction. But even more important, I felt about the world in general an innate sense of uselessness very difficult to explain or account for. Where, for instance, was I going in this heat? And what promise was there, really, of a good time in the streets? Though a moment before I seemed to have been propelled by emotions too fresh and too strong to disentangle, I now felt an inertia creeping back into my limbs. I felt the physical discomfort as an addition to the already accumulated, though as yet unassessed, spiritual discomforts of the soul, as though I had been absorbing the hot stickiness of the humid air through my pores.

On the beach, in the presence of the girl, though we did not exchange any words, I always felt charged with an abundant, conspiratorial energy. In those moments, life seemed rich and satisfying, a miracle of extraordinary beauty and wonder. Even the physical surroundings possessed for me their own unassembled beauty, even a touch of dignity. In the stones, in the buildings and recesses of the city there were mysteries of unweighed intelligences, and white people seemed to me to have a weight and strength quite unrelated to their potentialities as individuals. Simply the fact that they existed in the same world as the English girl, the fact that they ate in the same restaurants, rode the same buses, breathed the same air, gave them a share of humanity I would have denied to them, and I was prepared to forgive them their lack of significance.

22

Early next morning I was lying on the beach, watching the fishing boats casting out to sea over calm blue waters against a sky that was as pure as a chorister's smile, limpid like the steady gaze of a single vast, unblinking eye. Pure also was the early morning breeze, which carried the fresh odor of salt and seaweed. Against the hushed humid murmur of the sea, the traffic noises sounded distant, submerged. The motionless palms, the blurred city skyline still partially veiled in morning mist, the somber terraced houses on the distant hillside, everything, the whole unwaking world, seemed at peace. All but me. Beneath the sound of the constant drift and sigh of the waves, a music of metal struck at intervals from the loading ships in the wharves floated across the still inanimate air. But louder, more plaintive, was the ceaseless chant of my own quivering heart. The minutes ticked by. Watching, hoping, hoping, and watching, there was nothing for me to do but wait. Would she come? I tried to suppress my agitation, but could not avoid scanning the knoll of the hill where the English girl invariably came down, walking carelessly and dreamily in her dainty sandals to a place where she was accustomed to sunbathe, not too far from my "Non-White" side of the beach.

At ten o'clock the beach was still as deserted as a vast cheerless graveyard. Then as if the sea had suddenly been stirred by a powerful hand, it began to swell and froth, shaking and trembling like a huge mountain that was constantly breaking up and reforming. At intervals the waves broke upon the shore with a roar as elemental as the beating of blood in my own feverish veins, harsh, murderous, deranged.

While I listened to the boom and crash of the sea, listening as though to the beat of blood in my own heart, I saw the girl walking down toward the beach in short, mincing steps, like someone afraid to step over broken glass. She was dressed in a red-and-yellow flowered, off-the-shoulder dress of some soft flimsy material and a pair of red roman sandals, straps secured far above her ankles, focusing the eye on the clean sweep of her long, shapely legs. Without so much as a nod, let alone a murmured

"Good morning" (which I would not have expected, at any rate), she stumbled past me to her favorite roosting place near the legendary billboard with its mocking warning: BATHING AREA—FOR WHITES ONLY.

Here she first spread the towel over the ground before nonchalantly removing her dress to lie down for a while in her bikini, endlessly turning her body over and over in order to get the full benefit from the sun. For the first half hour she ignored me totally. She had brought with her some magazines whose pages she turned over listlessly, with a bored, discontented look. Occasionally, she stared at the sea as if she saw in it the vision of a possible escape, and with her diminished profile, the mouth drawn into an incurious dropping curve, she had the air of someone preoccupied with thoughts that were not entirely benign. After a little while she got up with the swift resolve of a child who suddenly remembers a game that promises unusual diversion. Quickly she pulled a swimming cap over her hair and glided toward the edge of the water where she first tested the temperature by dipping in her toes and wriggling them fearsomely. After this small dramatic prologue and without too much warning, she leapt suddenly under an incoming wave.

She was a good swimmer, bold, swift, confident, but fluid in all her movements. As if she were cork, a drifting piece of wood, the water tossed her about. She bobbed up and down, floated, rode perilously over another incoming wave before she disappeared altogether. Where she had been there was nothing to see but the calm surface of a very deep blue sea. It was with a mild sensation of shock therefore that I suddenly saw her emerge from the ocean, her bronzed limbs glistening with water, very near where I lay sunning myself on the white sands. Very calculated, I thought, with anger, following the animal grace of her lithe figure as she walked back across the little gurgling stream to her side of the beach without so much as an acknowledgment of my existence.

This must end, I thought, something must happen. Her indifference was beginning to rile me, and I longed to do something odd, unexpected and foolhardy to smash the facade of propriety that enclosed us both but that could not release us from our individual torment. In my frustration, with nothing better to do than gaze all day at the girl who would stay always beyond my reach, hemmed in and protected by all the laws that keep the races apart in our country, I began to plot the ways in which I could attract her attention without attracting the attention of the other white bathers who were beginning to accumulate in small groups all over the beach, but who unlike the solitary English girl always kept a safe distance from our nonwhite beach. I tried everything I could think of: some athletic exercises, a few spectacular somersaults, perfectly silly contortions, cartwheels, everything short of standing on my woolly head in the sands, in order to attract the girl's attention. I even dove into the water to execute some desperately impossible maneuvers that would have surely earned a round of applause at any aquatic display. For all the trouble I took, I received no more of an acknowledgment than if I had been a performing animal in a circus. Nothing would move the girl to pay any more serious attention to my display than she did a little later to the antics of a small dog that ran streaking ahead of its master, chasing a rubber ball it went to retrieve rather adroitly when it rolled into the sea. Balked, baffled, and deflated, I began to reflect that this was the sort of game a girl like Veronica knew well how to play. After all, manipulating men, even if by affecting this absurdly bored indifference, was her business. The memory of that fat white man with a blunt, moronic face flashed across my mind. He, too, was the victim of Veronica's whims. I remembered Veronica's easy lie in reply to the man's troubled question as to whether or not she knew me, "How am I expected to know every stray native who happens to hang around?" She had replied dishonestly, peevishly, shamelessly. It was a bold lie told carelessly without compunction, in the full knowledge that I had no power to contradict her. Girls like her would always get away with murder!

While I watched her through the hot glow of late morning sunshine, I started to hum an old song to myself. *If you don't like my gate, why do you swing on it! If you don't like my tree, why do you pick my peaches!* She was still gazing out to sea, still pretending to be unaware of my presence, when quite suddenly she began to ease the straps of her bra down from her shoulders, offering as usual a quick tantalizing view of her round, swollen breasts tipped with brown where the white flesh formed the succulent points of her nipples. Having finished this operation, conducted with the self-effacing modesty of a movie star on parade, she rolled over on her stomach, with the mounds of her inconvenient breasts squashed flat under her. Only then, as if to say "How about that for a quick glimpse," did she cast a swift inquiring glance in my direction. This mild self-exposure had been for me, apparently. I was convinced of this fact as soon as I saw the merest suggestion of a smile hovering around her slack, sensual lips, with that insidious but alluring look of random lust.

For me it was the signal, that mischievous, sudden twitch of a smile. In that sunburnt visage, calm and distracted, I saw anew a presentiment of my own pain. Transfixed, I watched the quick flare of that smiling expression, careless like a matchstick swiftly struck and quickly flung away into the darkness, a smile in which was blended in equal measure a certain amount of native cunning and concupiscence. I noticed the smoldering green eyes, which in a brief twinkle became shot with yellow and purple, while the pupils stayed fixed as if two bright pennies had been stuck into the holes where the eyes should have been. With those slanted, preternatural eyes she kept me fixed like a wriggling worm pinned against a wall. I stared back defensively, as helpless as if I had been pierced to the very core of my soul by her steady, serpentine gaze. I could do nothing but stare back. I was completely mesmerized. The heat itself added to my feeling of nervous discomfort without alleviating a growing excitement between us. For minutes on end we stared deliberately into each other's eyes. Obviously, if we could not use words we could use looks. Eyes. Meaningful gestures. It was all we had. With our eyes, we could make love as it soon became apparent. With our eyes, we could tell each other stories. With our eyes, we could protest each other's infidelities, the misery of our separation, our being artificially kept apart.

Then all of a sudden something incredible happened, something Veronica had never done before! While she kept her eyes fixed on mine, her mouth began to move, slowly at first, hesitantly, but later on more daringly, with the clear intention of arousing an answering response from me. She worked the mouth into spasms of coition in which was gathered all the gripping tension of limbs fusing into a final sexual embrace. I was startled by the bluntness of her message. With her wide painted, half-open mouth she formed the shape of an egg, a zero, an omega. She pouted, she thrust her lips outwardly in the shape of a kiss, her eyes gleaming with that avid lust that transforms a woman at the moment of orgasm into an abject animal. I, too, abruptly felt released from my cautious reserve. This was certainly a game two could play. Into that salivating circular shape she kept held out to me from a distance of only fifteen yards, I imagined myself thrusting my wet tongue. Insolently, taking my cue from her provocative example, I projected my tongue through my own pouted lips, then indecently rolled it round and round in a wretched imitation of a sexual organ gone berserk. Veronica, watching me keenly, her electric eyes growing larger and more elastic by the minute, began to move her hips ever so slowly, like a belly dancer rolling obscenely in response to the lewd suggestions of an invisible sheik. She moved undulatingly, indelicately, but also with such incredible subtlety that anyone observing us at a distance of twenty yards could not have realized what was going on.

She was lying on her side, facing me. I, on my side of

the beach, lay facing her. As she rolled the muscles of her stomach, she kept her gaze steadily fixed on mine. By now her eyes had become pure liquid and seemed to swim out at me like a pair of moist oyster shells. It was a performance to undermine anyone's intelligence. Indecorous, arousing, unexpectedly, maliciously tormenting. Beads of sweat broke from my face, my back was arched like a boar ready to strike. Veronica's mouth opened into a gleaming smile of malignant knavish sensuality, during which her pink tongue moved caressingly over her bright flashing teeth. She kept up her slow rotating movement in a grave discomposing imitation of sexual copulation, a grinding gyrating movement of the hips, which brought me to the crest of demented lust. Sometimes her hand brushed an invisible fly from the crotch of her small bikini and lingered there for a while before she would start to caress herself, again and again, ever so lightly, still rolling her hips, her stomach, in a strange trancelike indolent movement, a crazy sexual dance without parallel. By this time I was nearly delirious! For the first time, the girl was offering her body to me as plainly as if she had uttered the words of surrender. A perfect stripper she must have been. It showed in the skill with which she touched herself in her unhurried, methodical way, caressing first her arms, then the tips of her breasts, her flat stomach, down to her long shapely legs, which she raised, one at a time, her hands as light as a feather, swift in that quivering pagan motion of astounding primitive sensuality, while she continued to keep her eyes fixed on me in a kind of a mocking hypnotic gaze.

This was too much for me. I could no longer contain the tension. Oh, unnatural vices! Oh, vanity of all vanities!

The shame and disgrace of it! My member had grown absolutely rigid with a weak, purposeless passion. To say the very least, Veronica had already noticed the state of play, as they say, and this seemed to drive her mad with excitement. When I began to move as well, when both of us began to move together in a tense, grinding rhythm of unpremeditated sexual violence, mobilized by the force of a yearning so strong that neither of us had any thought who was watching or if someone was watching how to stop ourselves from that degrading pantomime of sex without contact, something inside my head seemed to break like a storm, something that for too long had remained threatening, an explosion of incalculable force that shook me to the very foundations! Simultaneously, Veronica uttered a sound from her throat like a strangled animal, the whites of her eyes turning upward like two eggs on a saucer, and I saw her body reeling as if racked by a gigantic tremor. We came together, dragged by the retching flesh across the space of prohibition and taboo that separated us. I could see the force of Veronica's orgasm in the cruel distortion of her face. I could see it in the way she collapsed suddenly on the towel, clutching her belly and writhing as if trying to free herself from a cramp that would not release its hold upon her, until after what seemed an eternity she lay still like a crushed animal, her eyes changing color.

Gradually, as though finally overcome by the sun and the wanton excesses of our bestial games, Veronica fell asleep. As for me, it was not very difficult to tell something untoward had happened. The evidence was as material as if I had purposefully brought myself to a climax. That is how it was between Veronica and me. *Apartheid?* We had defeated apartheid. We had finally perfected a method of making love without even making contact, utilizing empty space like two telepathic media exchanging telegraphic messages through the sexual airwaves.

23

In court, Veronica lied. She lied with so much ease, with so little effort, that my first reaction was one of stunned disbelief. Even more surprising was her swanlike grace and beauty, passionate and mysterious, so that when she walked into the witness box she looked like a trembling, rocking bird, sleek and fine-feathered, her eyes blank and prostrate like those of a wounded animal. They were without doubt the eyes of a victim and they drew naturally around her the angry sympathy of all the white people who crowded into the public galleries.

She spoke at length of the weather, of her physical paralysis in that incredible heat. She described in minute detail the clothes she was wearing, her flimsy undergarments, her understandable eagerness to slip out of them. Vividly, painstakingly, she painted an attractive picture of her dainty, picturesque bungalow, of its unfortunate solitariness, of her isolation from any form of social intercourse. She spoke of her love of the sea, of its great healing power, of her inextinguishable passion for it. "On the afternoon in question, Your Lordships," Veronica testified, "I had just returned from a swim at the beach. It was so hot, as I recall, that when I reached my bungalow all I could think of was how soon I should get out of my clothes, to sort of cool down. Sweat was simply pouring out of every pore of my body. Even the clothes I was wearing were quite damp, clinging to my body. I felt absolutely crushed under the weight of the sun. When I got to my bungalow, I couldn't even see the steps leading to my door because of the dazzle in my eyes. I remember that as soon as I entered the door I began to slip off my clothes," Veronica confided. "I didn't know what I was doing or anything. I just sort of let them drop one by one wherever I happened to be at the moment without bothering to pick them up. My dress, my bra, my pants. It was all so nice and cool in my living room I just flung myself on the bed exactly as I was, completely in the raw."

Kakmekaar looked most unhappy at Veronica's eagerness to dwell on physical details. His purpose, apparently, was to present her to the court and the public as the perfect symbol of a stainless purity, modest, virtuous, bashful. Veronica, it seemed, had other ideas, other preoccupations.

She gave the impression of someone who took particular delight in alluding to the most intimate details of her toilette. While she spoke, building up a picture of intemperate weather, of her own sensual agony and physical abandon, the men peered down from the public galleries, several of them struggling fiercely to get a better view of her figure. Kakmekaar frowned. "Did you not close down after you when you entered the bungalow, Miss Slater?"

Veronica gave a faint smile. "Well, Your Lordships, I was in a complete daze, as you can imagine. I am not normally a very careless person about things such as leaving a door open while I am undressing, but I suppose I was too hot really to think. Even the Met Office people said it was the hottest day they could remember in twenty-two years. Birds were falling off the rooftops. I must've lost any sense of modesty." She looked just then as if she were preparing to slip out of her clothes again. Such was the power of her magical spell that the more incredible her lies became, the more fascinated I became with her. While she gave her evidence, I never tired of watching this white woman to whom I was tied as much by a tissue of fantasies and lies as by our painfully interrupted coitus. Standing in that witness box, calm, lucid, almost joyful in her ability to invent her fictions, she looked like a woman eternally consumed by some invisible fire.

Kakmekaar consulted his notes, flipping rapidly through a number of pages, each time wetting his finger before turning the page. He paused and looked at the girl. "Did you then fall asleep during this time, Miss Slater?" Kakmekaar solicited.

"Oh, yes, I *must* have done, Your Lordships!"

Veronica promptly answered. "Most certainly! I must have completely flagged out because I don't remember much of what happened next until I was woken up by a noise of something moving about the room. I thought I was dreaming! Suddenly there was this native standing over my bed, his eyes looking sort of wild and crazy, like he'd just seen a most enchanting succubus! At first I didn't know what to think. Was I seeing things or what? Well, honestly, I couldn't believe it! Horror of horrors! There I was, stark naked, in the middle of this vast unmade bed and all of a sudden, out of nowhere, a native man was staring down at me as if I were a piece of mutton or something! I was so shocked I didn't even have time to think to cover myself!"

Veronica was an accomplished storyteller, with a considerable grasp of human psychology. Evidently she possessed an instinctive knowledge of what constituted audience appeal. A lively sense of timing, an ingenious and subtle faculty for creating suspense, and, when the occasion demanded it, an adequate preparation of her audience for scenes of great climactic power were part of her virtuosity. As a narrator, she was quite simply magnificent. As a living example, the brutalized victim of male lust, she was superb. In her presentation of the so-called facts relating to our monumental carnal struggle that afternoon in the desperate seclusion of her bungalow, she was wildly, outrageously inventive, garrulous, inexhaustible. The judges, the lawyers, the black and white spectators in the public galleries were visibly stirred by the vision of a lonely desperate white woman menaced by grave dangers. The atmosphere in the dimly lit court was one of hushed expectation interrupted only by the buzz of prurient excitement when Veronica's description of her sexual violation became too graphic to pass without at least a murmur of surprise.

"I tried to scream, of course," Veronica remembered, I thought rather belatedly. She repeated the words as someone might do who had stumbled on an interesting insight. "I tried to scream but no sound came out of my mouth. The whole thing was simply beyond the wildest nightmare. Even now my skin crawls when I think of it! There I was, absolutely dazed by heat, and when I wake up, there is this native running his fingers over my body, caressing my skin like a great musical virtuoso playing on the strings of a violin!"

A few individuals who found this image unexpectedly diverting sniggered under their sleeves. "Silence in Court!" a court orderly yelled. In acknowledgment of this timely intervention, Veronica gave a kind of nod before continuing. "Well, Your Lordships, I could see the native was getting quite excited by now, his breath was coming out in short gasps as if he had been running a long time. For the first time I was really scared. My throat felt completely dry. I was very much aware that I was in great danger and this was confirmed to me when the native suddenly became threatening. By this time he had his hand wedged firmly between my legs. When he saw I was about to scream he shoved me down and yelled in my face, 'Don't make a sound, or I'll kill you!' Those were the very words he used. He had something in his hand which looked like a knife and I was convinced he meant what he said."

Veronica was a fantasist by nature. In that witness box she was brilliant, dazzling, the voice harshly metallic and mellifluent by turns; her shuddering white flesh seemed to undulate before our very eyes. Once again I surrendered to that vision of the girl on the beach, moving her lips in perfect rhythm to mine; I heard again the stifled orgasmic cry like the strangled whimper snatched from the back of the throat of a dying animal. I was also enchanted by the intense expression in her face, which resembled the passionate absorption of an artist in a moment of self-creation.

"Did this native male say what he wanted from you, Miss Slater?" Kakmekaar's voice seemed to come from a distance, soft, languid, cajoling. "I mean, did he seem to you like someone looking for a job, perhaps?"

Veronica first looked surprised at the question. Then she looked immemorially solitary, abandoned, exceptionally ill-used. "Oh, no, Your Lordships!" she retorted. "Far from it. A job was the last thing he was looking for! I know because I asked him what he wanted from me and he didn't even bother to answer. I said, 'What do you want?' very frightened by now, and the native just looked at me and grinned. It was a ghastly grin like the grimace of a wild animal and he just kept on touching me, playing with one of my breasts, feeling me up. I'll never forget his eyes. They looked as if they were about to pop out of his head. His throat was moving as if he was finding great difficulty in swallowing. At other times he ran his tongue hungrily over his ashy lips, sort of smacking a bit as if he couldn't believe his luck." At this point, Veronica suddenly paused as if unable to go on until Kakmekaar spoke again encouragingly. "Go on, Miss Slater. I know this whole incident must be extremely distressing to you, but you've got to tell his Lordships what happened.

"Well, after this everything was a nightmare. The native started to undress himself. When I realized what he was preparing to do, I was so frightened I began to shake like a leaf! I pleaded with him not to do anything. I told him he could take anything from the house, only to leave me alone. And, of course, by this time I was sobbing and I don't know what else, pleading with him to please take anything at all but to leave me alone. To my absolute horror, the native responded by pulling out his huge black thing, sort of rubbing it gleefully with the palm of his hand, getting it ready for action, I suppose; well, my blood just froze into ice. I must've vomited then. Everything suddenly became completely *black!* I couldn't bear the idea of him shoving that thing inside me! But there was no stopping him then. Slobbering and frothing at the mouth, he was practically throwing himself about on top of me, forcing my legs apart, pushing and pushing! Oh, God, it was just horrible!" Veronica shuddered, then cradling her head in her arms she slumped over the witness box, sobbing uncontrollably. It was a magnificent performance. A number of white men rose as if preparing to leap over the public galleries in order to get at my black carcass, but they were shoved back to their seats by vigilant court orderlies. There were mumbled cries of *"Jou vuil bobbejaan!* You dirty baboon!" Others were crying, "Lynch the *donderse kaffer!"*

This story, only a grain of which contained any truth whatsoever, was received with stunned silence by the court. Even Kakmekaar seemed completely overwhelmed by the enormity of my crime in defiling the body of a white woman with such ruthless violence. Gazing at Veronica, the fat prosecutor seemed paralyzed for a while by the extent of that girl's ordeal at the hands of a native violator. When he finally shook himself from the powerful vision of incarnate evil, he mopped his brow repeatedly with a handkerchief that was already soaking with sweat. "Let me finally ask you this question, Miss Slater," Kakmekaar sighed wearily. "The defense will attempt to persuade this court to believe," Kakmekaar said indignantly, referring to my defense lawyer's preliminary remarks in his opening statement, "that you, Miss Slater, were acquainted with the accused, that, in fact, your conduct led the native accused to believe that you welcomed his attention; indeed, that you, Miss Slater, invited this ghastly attack upon yourself. What would you say to that?"

"That is a wicked lie!" Veronica replied stiffly, turning her gaze impassively upon the dock where I sat, astonished by her instant unhesitating denial. When our eyes met for a brief second, Veronica's gaze did not falter, did not waver. A minute later, she looked appealingly at Kakmekaar, the prosecutor, whose very face seemed to ridicule any suggestion, however slight, that a white woman could ever enter into sexual complicity with a native. The judges, too, looked distressed by the allegation. Visibly emboldened by these signs of white solidarity, Veronica concluded on a confident note. "Your Worship, I have never set eyes upon this native before. It's quite possible, of course, that he might have followed me around without my being aware of it. Your Lordships, I am not in the habit of studying the face of every native who crosses my path!"

"Just so, Miss Slater! Just so!" Kakmekaar responded encouragingly. The folds of flesh beneath the prosecutor's sleepy eyes were puffed up like swelling dough, emphasizing the funeral pallor of his face. "So you deny ever having seen this native male hanging around on the beach where you were accustomed to bathe?"

"I deny it!"

"You deny ever having exchanged a single word, Miss Slater, a single look, of having offered any form of encouragement that might have led the accused to—?"

She never allowed Kakmakaar to finish, "I deny it!" she said resolutely, decisively, without the slightest hesitation in her voice. I was amazed. Her lying, which was done with such a marvelously cool audacity, had the same fascination for me that the most brazen display of evil and corruption can sometimes exert on even the most confirmed saint and believer. Again I was struck by how stunningly beautiful she looked in her knitted white dress and white coat and sloppy, wide-brimmed hat, tilted at an angle over one eye, a vision of purity even more beguiling for having been tampered with, as the prosecution was now alleging. But beneath the brim of that sloppy hat, what was visible of the girl's face was abnormally, translucently white. The eyes were ringed by dark circles of torment and fatigue as if she had not slept very well the night before. Nevertheless, throughout the cross-examination, her calm stoicism and regal poise had remained absolutely indestructible. As I remember now, only once when she narrated the distressing circumstances of her body's violation had the voice dropped so low that Kakmekaar, in spite of his unfailing gallantry and solicitousness, had been obliged to urge the witness to put more effort into her answers. "Speak up, Miss Slater, speak up," he had encouraged her, "so that Your Lordships can hear what you have to say. Did you ever at any time participate in the sorts of orgies that it is being alleged by the defense have sometimes taken place in a certain house in Norwood?''

"Orgies?'' Veronica repeated. The faintest hint of a smile curved her upper lip: "What sort of orgies? I have never participated in any orgies in my whole life.'' Although I had adequate knowledge of English, it was the unalterable law of the South African courts that whenever a native stood trial, an interpreter had to be provided in order to translate into African languages the minutest details of the proceedings, but in this instance the African brother who made the most valiant attempts to render into my native Zulu tongue all that was being said in English soon experienced difficulties. The tangled web of erotic perversion woven into the evidence soon became too much for him to comprehend, let alone translate into another language. "Orgies?'' the interpreter repeated uncertainly. "Your Lordship, there is no word for 'orgies' in the Zulu language.''

"Good Gracious, man! Are you trying to tell this court that your people had never heard of *orgies* before the white man came to this continent?'' Justice De Klerk made the question sound like an indictment. The interpreter, who was standing next to me supposedly in order to translate what was being said, looked crestfallen. I took the opportunity to save him from further embarrassment by leaning over the dock and whispering into his ear, *"Ama-orgies, mos, kulapha bedlana khona abelungu, beganga bonke! Bephuzana nangemlomo njengezinja!''*

The interpreter at first looked flabbergasted. Quite likely he suspected that I was playing him an unseemly joke. He looked around him hesitantly as if to appeal for aid.

Then presumably deciding to throw all caution to the wind, he gave the court a wide foolish grin and then stood facing the African gallery. "The big baas asks if the madam was in the habit of visiting a certain house where everyone *ate* and *drank* everyone else, copulating like dogs as if there was no tomorrow!" He finished, licking his tongue, and from the galleries to the left the Africans gave a collective murmur like a slow buzz of many disturbed bees. The women pressed their infants closely to their bosoms as if they feared such talk might affect them adversely in later life in some yet undetermined way.

"You deny ever having participated in any such orgies, Miss Slater?"

"Your Lordship, I feel quite insulted at even the suggestion!"

"Just so, Miss Slater! Just so!" Kakmekaar repeated complacently. "Indeed, Your Lordships, it is our submission that the entire suggestion that the complainant has been associated in any way with such sordid practices is an unworthy attempt by the defense at character assassination. It's a complete fabrication, an attempt by the defense to besmirch the character of a young woman who has not only suffered physical assault of the most distasteful kind in the hands of a native sex maniac, but who from now on must carry the stigma and psychological scars such an assault is bound to leave on a sensitive nature."

Even for Max Siegfried Müller, a man with a normally equable temper, this imputation of deviousness and foul play was too much to bear. Before the judges could intervene, Müller was on his feet, flinging aside the prosecution charges, making counteraccusations of his own. In a voice tinged with disdain, he lashed out at Kakmekaar and his underlings until the fat prosecutor, looking like an aroused tousle-headed friar, stumbled to his feet, vainly protesting his innocence. Müller was not to be silenced so easily. "Your Lordships, My Learned Friend is the last person to instruct us in the ineffable ways of virtue. The conduct of the police and the prosecution in this case has been nothing short of scandalous. Improper pressure on the witnesses, inexplicable disappearances of files, and exhibits of extremely vital importance to the defense case—these have been the marked features of this case! By adopting these 'back-alley' methods, the prosecution is clearly hoping to intimidate us!"

At last Mr. Justice De Klerk, a frail figure in oversized scarlet robes, joined the uproar. "Mr. Müller, I won't have these unseemly exchanges between counsel take place in my court."

"If the Court pleases," Müller surrendered with surly displeasure. After a brief silence, Chief Justice De Klerk demanded further clarification. "Mr. Müller, are you intending to lead evidence linking this witness with certain alleged practices in an address in Norwood?"

"Your Lordship, let me make this clear. We would have preferred to spare the court these unsavory revelations, but, frankly, the sanctimonious attempts by the prosecution to elevate the character of this complainant to one of almost mystical piety and stainless spirituality is such patent humbug that we have no choice but to produce witnesses who will testify, not only to the truth of the allegations we have made, but witnesses, My Lords, who will provide sufficient evidence in the form of videotape films and other photographic exhibits showing beyond any doubt that far from being the irreproachable incarnation of virtue and unsullied chastity, the complainant has been a frequent participant in perversions of the most indescribable nature."

After that, the uproar was unbelievable! It was a little before lunch break when Max Siegfried Müller made this unexpected intervention. For one second, a deep crushing silence descended upon the court, a single moment in which the major players in this sordid drama seemed to be reduced to a numbed inertness. Then pandemonium broke loose. A loud incredulous murmur rose from the galleries: Müller, Kakmekaar, the judges, they all began talking at the same time. The ladies and gentlemen of the press, like a pack of hyenas roused from insensible stupor, dashed from their seats to the door in a collective stampede, howling and jostling one another for first place at the telephones. Doubtless the headlines for the evening dailies were already in the making: RAPED ENGLISHWOMAN TOOK PART IN ORGIES, ADVOCATE ALLEGES! Another headline, which I saw only a week later, even contrived to suggest a link between the so-called rape and the wild Norwood parties. WHITE WOMAN RAPED AFTER ORGIES, DEFENSE ALLEGES.

The story I told to the court, to the judge, and his assessors was essentially the same story I have been telling here off and on; the same story I later told to Emile Dufré, to my mother, to my friends and my relatives. But in telling and retelling it to the court I found in the end that the whole thing had become somewhat garbled, confused, it had lost any clear logical outline, had become a story without any apparent shape or form, like a modern novel whose plot resembles the shapelessness of emotion itself. In such novels, things happen but the causes remain unclear. The ending is often said to lie concealed in the very beginning, but to discover in what this beginning consists is not such a simple matter, believe me. Dufré ought to know. Since his arrival in the country, he has been trying without noticeable success to trace the origins of what he is pleased to call the "pathology of my condition."

On the last day, the day of judgment, I had walked into the crowded court surrounded by a host of armed guards, my mind blank and curiously detached as though I were about to witness the climax in the life of someone else; the same feeling of detachment, I suppose, that had possessed me during that last unintelligible encounter with Veronica in the bungalow, the same blank, stupid gaze I imagine with which I had regarded the prostrate figure of the girl on her high brass bed. Having been pushed, or half jostled into the dock, I dropped down on the bench, stared impassively at the crowded court until I caught a glimpse of the stooped, stumbling figure of my mother approaching from the door, already in black mourning clothes, covered up in a blanket. With her were the three aunts and two younger uncles who had traveled all night from Eshowe to be present during the last day of the trial. Each uncle flanked the bowed figure, each had given her an arm for support.

As the small band led by the redoubtable Ma-Mlambo advanced slowly from outdoor sunlight into the lamplit gloom of the vast court, I noted how each face looked solemnly, painfully bewildered, almost as if each owner had been called upon without notice, without justification, to stand trial for the vile crime of rape. I found the sight of my mother in such obvious distress particularly moving; but painful, too, was the knowledge that it was *my* behavior, *my* outlandish lust and ambition, that was responsible for these people's immense confusion and distress.

Nothing is exactly like the gorgeous panoply of a South African court: the mock ceremony, the pretense, the play-acting. South Africa is a country in which every principle of justice has been tampered with, debased, even reversed; a country where truth, fairness, and magnanimity have been chucked out of the window, and only the shell of intricate procedure remains; a country of the memory of empty ritual, of "Mi-Lord," "Your Honor"; a country of "My Learned Friend is pleased to cite the case of Neville vs. Kumalo, but what about Chief Justice Sommerville's ruling in the case of Gubase vs. Lavabo?" Elegant form, gorgeous ceremony, empty ritual. It is all that remains to haunt the memory of those who grew up in better times, when the fiction of impartial justice toward black and white was still vigorously maintained. Now all that is over and forgotten; embarrassing, too, one can imagine, the memory of law as a passion for justice. For something has replaced this passion with an eerie, faintly barbarous, and oppressive atmosphere. That combination of barbarity and oppression could be detected in the very atmosphere of the court proceedings, a stifling, fetid air of violence let off by damp, rancid flesh confined too long in a tight khaki uniform. It could be discerned in the coarse red faces, in the eyes in which a massive monumental brutality slumbered like a crouching beast, ready to spring. Even the judges in their scarlet robes, gloomy-faced, hawk-eyed, constantly leaning forward to catch the minutest inflection in the voices of the lawyers, conveyed this impression of bloodthirstiness, having abandoned any pretense to their former expansive generosity. Only Kakmekaar appeared in a new light, profoundly self-possessed, even meditative. Contrary to his former blustering tactics, he now contrived to look inexpressibly bored. To the end, Kakmekaar was playing the game with consummate skill.

Two days before, the corpulent state representative had presented a different face to the public, more ferocious, more bitingly contemptuous. Once or twice, while I tried to describe Veronica's unorthodox behavior, her provocative exhibitionistic self-displays, Kakmekaar had swiveled round in his chair to share his incredulity with members of the public. Once, when I offered the view during the cross-examination that I thought Veronica had derived unusual gratification from being observed by a native without her clothes on, Kakmekaar had roared his contemptuous disapproval. "You think a white madam can feel flattered by being gazed at by a baboon like you!" The judges, conscious to the very end of their duty to a certain conception of justice, however vague and abstract, had murmured warningly, "Mr. Kakmekaar! Mr. Kakmekaar!" Only my defense lawyer, Max Siegfried Müller, his memories of German concentration camps still intact, appeared controlled, solemnly measured in speech, disgusted but not surprised by all the pantomime of crime and punishment.

At times I felt quite alone up there in the dock, surrounded by hostile white faces, pitied by the black ones, a lamb being prepared for slaughter. People drifted in, the orderlies moved about in creaking shoes, heads turned my way without warning, frequently came together in muffled gossip, which carried right across the well of the court. Above all, there was the light, white, searing, and blinding, which filtered through a side window of the court, a light strong enough to dazzle the eyes. It was the only light that had seemed to relieve the gloom of the court, but now it seemed suddenly menacing, powdery white in an unnatural way. It was an accursed, pestilential light, lacking the rich, nourishing velvety density of darkness itself. Veronica, sitting in the front row, her hands folded neatly upon her straight lap, appeared to be wrapped up in this harsh devilish light. She looked like a ghost shut up in the oppressive friendless glow of a satanic eternal white night, a phantom produced by my own unreleased nightmares now certain to bring about my ruin. I remember being called upon to stand, being urged to swear to tell the truth, nothing but the truth, and hearing a man I could not see, an English-speaking white man bellowing at the top of his voice across the vast silent courtroom, "Bloody rapist kaffir bastard! Why not cut off his filthy black dingus, the rotten swine!"

Commotion followed this outburst. Perhaps fearing a sudden outbreak of unexpected violence, a clutch of white orderlies moved quickly toward the vague figure in dark blazer and gray flannels. Flailing hands shot out, a scuffle ensued, the judges issued their warning. At last overcome by a feeling like nausea, my mind struggling fiercely but impotently in the darkness of that white mist, I could no longer make out what was going on. By now I was in the grip of a dread so deep and overwhelming it was no use trying to keep my mind on the proceedings. Why not let events take their course? Let the mind drift where it willed.

While I stood clutching at the edges of the witness box,

I was conscious of Max Siegfried Müller standing by my side, gently urging me to tell the court what happened. "Tell the Lordships everything," Müller pleaded, "exactly how it happened, Mr. Sibiya. Don't be shy." As Chief Justice De Klerk himself had already pointed out, this was the great moment, after all, when I had to speak up for myself, when I had to create the right impression, the moment when I had to vindicate myself; but how could I make the judges or anyone else believe me when I no longer knew what to believe myself? There was the English girl herself I was supposed to have violated, calmly sitting in the front row of a court that was solidly packed with spectators, a girl looking extremely cool, radiant, unblinking, looking, in fact, as sweetly inviolate as a freshly blossomed flower. Steady, luminous, her skin shedding luster as brilliant as the noonday light, she seemed to be beyond the profane touch of sensual appetite.

"Mr. Sibiya, tell His Lordship!" Müller patiently prodded. "Did you rape this lady, whom you heard just now described as the helpless victim of a brutal assault?" I tried to respond but could think of nothing to say. The tongue seemed to cleave to the roof of my mouth. Well, had I raped the girl or not? What in God's name had happened during that fateful afternoon when, having followed the girl from the beach to her small bungalow on the edge of the industrial wastelands, I had observed this girl calmly standing in the center of the room as though arrested in the middle of a profound thought. Once having entered her bungalow, half deranged and seething with a voluptuous fever, how had I come to lose my senses so nearly completely that indifferent to the thought of neighbors or the ever-watchful police, I had lain hands on the body of a white woman with whom I had not exchanged more than half a dozen words in the doorway of a tobacco shop? Only the girl, Veronica herself, could have supplied the missing links in my faulty and, no doubt, hopelessly affected memory. Nevertheless, it was just this girl who could not now be trusted, who had managed to weave a web of fiction so completely divorced from the truth that, paradoxically, it seemed the more credible for being so entirely a work of a diseased fabulist imagination. After all, just because it was so completely a work of fiction it was also the least likely to offend the intelligence of our seasoned judges who yearn for the kind of evidence that fits their prejudices. What right-thinking judge, for example, could believe that, in a country like ours, a white woman in full possession of her senses could take off all her clothes while being observed by a black stranger; and that having taken off her clothes in the presence of this black man, this same girl could continue to lie naked and untroubled on the bed while the man, who was no doubt preparing to violate her, stood gazing down at her outstretched body? The whole thing was simply incredible.

In court that morning, during both my main evidence and the cross-examination, I went over the same old ground again and again, urged on by the judges, by Kakmekaar the prosecutor, by the defense. I explained how after the tumult of our mock copulation on the beach, I had followed the girl across the yellow sand dunes, up the small beach path to the main road that runs from north to south; and having crossed it, I had traversed the empty wasteland behind the gliding figure, keeping steady pace behind the girl's soft-flowing movements, each step more fateful than the one before, until she turned into the gate of the green-painted bungalow set against a clump of trees. I remember the weather was magnificent that day. It was quite breathtaking to behold the dark nervous shimmer of sun upon the dark foliage—the pale air rising blond and dazzling as though a million needles were scattering through the air. I had an intense conviction that the girl was aware of being followed. More than once she had turned round to favor me with one of her mocking mischievous glances. When she finally entered the gate, mounting each step as if she were climbing the very cross upon which she would yet be crucified, there had been in her movements, in her smooth sun-soaked limbs, the staggering hesitant weariness of someone ready to collapse at the very first moment she found something upon which to sit or lie.

Having let herself into the room, she did not immediately shut the door. From where I was standing near the front gate I had a view of almost the entire front room, of the big double bed on one side and the chest of drawers in the further corner, of the large mirror that occupied the empty space above the chest of drawers and the small table with a bowl of freshly cut flowers on it. The windows and the curtains were thrown open and a macabre ghostly white light seemed to pour into the room, emphasizing the narrow area of light from that of the immense, brooding shadow. Even from that distance I felt the hot, sticky intimacy of the room as though I myself were moving about in it. Struggling to reconstruct what I remembered of the inside of that bungalow from my recent break-in, I tried to picture in my mind's eye the disposition of every object in the room: the table, the chairs, and beyond the door leading into the sunlit kitchen, the bathroom with the gleaming rail of steel upon which hung her sheerest nylon underclothes. Tense, breathless, unable to still the rapid beating of my heart, I followed the girl's movement like a man in a daze, yet remained firmly rooted to the ground on which I stood.

Still within view, Veronica dropped her beach bag on the floor and sat for a moment on the edge of the wide bed, rocking up and down like someone testing the durability of the springs for some dark purpose. Using one foot against the heel of the other, she kicked off her shoes. Then she became animated, as though she had suddenly thought of something very interesting to do. I watched her pass from the living room area into the kitchen only to reappear munching a fruit, whose oozing slimy juice dripped down the side of her mouth like dark stains of wine, forcing her to pass the back of her hand swiftly across her liquid red lips.

She paused, scanning the front yard as far as the gate. Throughout, her movements were languid, weary, sullen, as though zeal and devotion to her body had become too much even for her, who all day long did not seem to have anything to do but minister to its needs. After all, eating, swimming, and sleeping seemed to constitute the exact horizons of her day's activities. These activities included, I suppose, her prodigious lovemaking, for in my fantasies about the girl I imagined her lovemaking to be frantic, tireless, indefatigable. Frequently I thought of the fat Greek, of the house in Norwood, and the pink naked shapes moving perpetually against the lighted window. She, the center of my desire, the focus of all my eternal longing, my inexhaustible passion, was now standing before me, one hand on one hip, the other hip thrust outward in an outrageous, tormenting self-display.

About to turn away, she suddenly caught sight of my dark immobile figure leaning against the rickety gate, gazing at her with all the suppressed, irrational violence of my long-pent-up desire. Even at that distance she seemed to feel the concentrated force of my now fully aroused passion. Her body changed its posture, lost its calm breathless purity, became suddenly rigid. For a few seconds we gazed at each other, the distance between the door and the gate suddenly filled with such throbbing, aching desire that it was all that the girl and I could do to remain where we were.

At long last, Veronica turned as if to go, but she did not shut the door. I noticed she was doing something with her hands; narrow, flowing, gleaming like polished copper in the intense daylight heat of the little room, her naked arms were raised and she was fumbling with pins in her hair, which was falling down in shining cascades over her smooth shoulders.

Then, all at once, she did something else that startled me so much that, blinking incredulously against the dazzling afternoon sunshine, I did not at first believe my eyes were seeing properly. Swiftly, as though moved by an impulse that had to be obeyed without question, her face once more turning toward the door, she unhooked her dress. The dress dropped in a heap around her ankles. Left only with her bra and pants, she simply moved aside as if trying to avoid stepping on something. I have a clear memory of that exact moment, of the dead weight of flesh on my bones, the feverish beat of the blood at the top of my skull. Outside, the air smelled of stale perfume, a combination of damp heat and melting tar.

While I was trying to recover my surprise at this incredible display, the girl began to undo her bra! Like the magnificent stripper that she was, Veronica's hands were quick, nimble. Through the diaphanous haze of vibrating light I saw her half-nude body moving in a pale cloud that seemed to envelop her flesh like a tangle of hands caressing a nymphomanic goddess. Having flung her bra aside, with the gliding movements of a panther she began to slide out of her pants. Momentarily, I had to shut my eyes to steady my vision against what I was obliged to see. Veronica was standing in the middle of the floor, as naked as on the day she was born. The odd thing, when I think of it now, is that seeing a naked white body for the first time was not in itself as provocative as I had imagined it would be. It was, rather, the invitation implicit in the gesture that endowed the act of Veronica's disrobing with a peculiar erotic force, which passed through me with the glancing sharpness of a knife blade. In that small bungalow, surrounded by dense trees in which nothing, not even the smallest branch or blade of grass seemed to move, a naked white woman stood in the middle of her room in a mindless careless pose wrapped up in a shawl of light. She was like a burning flame, something of the devil placed there to lure me to my perdition. But such sweet alluring there never was to behold! Soft curves, long, tapering legs, a gold-tinted face. Parts of her flesh were smooth and glowing, giving the surface of her skin the shocking immediacy of a recently completed painting, pigment still fresh and vivid on the canvas. With her slim hands she cupped her breasts as though in their solemn rounded solidity they needed some form of support, then she pressed them together like two pieces of rubber before stepping over to the bed where she lay on top with nothing to cover her.

A pang shot through me; nausea seared my throat. I gulped for air. I swallowed. Sweat like morning dew broke from my brow. I know I should have fled that bungalow and that girl before something happened, but I did not. Like a river in flood, my lust swept me off toward that half-open door, toward the room in which the girl lay like a watchful lioness ready to spring. As though in a trance, I was running up those steps, hurrying toward the door and the now temporarily invisible body.

When I entered the room the English girl half rose from her vast bed, uttering a small cry of surprise as befits a solitary woman who finds herself suddenly confronted with a strange man in her room; to say nothing of a white woman, who naked as a newborn baby, wakes to find a native male staring down at her vulnerable white body. Yet the girl's cry was not really one of alarm. It was too perfunctory for that. She did not get off her bed and she gave no sign of wishing to do so. Instead, she lay on her back, staring up at me with her slanted green eyes in which I thought I saw fear struggling with the dominant impulse of a curious but random lust.

Now a breath from her skin came to me like the hot peppery smell of volcanic lava and brought back to me all the forgotten memories of dank, cloistered childhood odors, the milky smell of my mother's breasts, the warm damp odor of crumpled bedclothes. Casting a quick glance at the girl's face, I thought I saw in it a wild despair and something else too—a hot eagerness for what was impossible to give a name. At the moment when I knelt down beside her prostrate body, her eyes looked yearning and melancholy, as though in the movement of the merest shadow she saw a subtler kind of power she could not yet acquire for herself. In all that time, neither of us had spoken. Her mouth was open, and in the droop of her chin there was an edge of a lingering dissatisfaction.

I seized her then, seized her roughly with a long-stoked-up violence that was a halfway house of love, murder, and rape. I even enjoyed the swift mobile look of fear that shot across her face, but there was also in the depths of her eyes a perverse excitement. She groaned, she moaned softly. I think she actually believed I was going to strike her. But I didn't. I didn't strike her. Instead, I ran my free hand through her hair, down the side of her body, exploring its many planes and curves as a man does who is trying to find a way through some unknown and difficult territory. Then I lost control altogether! No longer able to contain my passion, I found myself hungrily, guiltily kissing her mouth, her face, her ears, her breasts, her arms. Our mouths mingled like water. I seized her again, lightly, by the throat—oh that white throat! Images came fleetingly to mind from the everlasting tragedy of Desdemona and the Moor. Hurriedly I licked the shadowless surface of that immaculate skin, slithering gradually down to the breasts, to the vivid bloom of their fragranced tumescence, descending finally from the rounded fleshiness of the torso to the surprising hollowness of the belly and the darkening swell of the hips.

Feeling my face dipping between the confines of her

creamy thighs, I heard the girl moan like a torn animal, grasping at my ears, my head, my hair, in order to impede further progress down to that turbulent foam of beach where the legs came together to form a windless gulf. Struggling fiercely, she pulled at my hair, but it was too short to offer a good handle. Then, just as suddenly, she ceased to struggle and grasping my head between her cool hands she at last drew me willingly into her fine arms, moving her mouth so soundlessly that the protest, if protest it was, was only a mute echo against my insatiable greed.

That was all. No speech, no pleas, no exhortations. Not even a scream to warn me off, although at one stage, while I was attempting to achieve penetration, we even rolled off the bed together onto the floor, the girl grappling with my belt, aiding and abetting that final entry into her windless harbor. When I entered her narrow cunt, I felt as if I had blundered into a dark secret room full of old forgotten treasures. She was hot, wet, already salivating down there, but the touch of her flesh had a raw, newer quality than anything I could remember. At the smallest contact with her skin, I was aware of something within her, an enormous vibrating sensation, which seeped through my own limbs and made them seem to possess a weight that was entirely novel to me. I could feel the skin stretched tight over my bones, my hair tightened around my skull, and an odd sensation like an electric shock passed through my body. My breath was coming out forced and wheezing, as though a heavy load were pressing down on my chest.

Veronica, I remember, made love with her eyes wide open, the violet pupils glinting with a surprised triumphant light as we moved together in a perfectly coordinated rhythm. Her face looked hot and flushed, suffused with a high brilliant color, something like white scum bubbling on her half-open mouth; flying strands of brown hair fell over her avid, sweat-moistened face, while a small perfume-reeking finger ran across my mouth in a strange gentle supplication, provoking a shudder of thrills down my spine like scuttling mice.

So this is what it had come to, this the torrid center of all the days and weeks of longing, my infernal need, my obsessions; this, the ecstatic unscrupulous ending of all my heretical, devilish dreams; this wonder, this excess, this festal music, this most amazing rush of passion, the haunting discordant lust as unreflecting as it was ferocious. Small detonations were going on inside my head. A nerve was throbbing wildly in my neck. I could hear blood beating like pulsating drums in my temples. But come what may, I was determined to reach my climax. Miraculously, the girl's body seemed to flow back into her white fragility, then back again into the black dimness of the room's shadow, until, struggling together across the floor, we rolled into a small patch of bright sunlight, and briefly I caught a glimpse of the girl's face: sharper now the flesh on her cheeks, too vivid the flesh around the mouth, her skin a little hot and flushed with that bitter allure that made the soft pink rim of her mouth look like the gill of a fish.

Far away, at a distance I could not measure, I thought I could hear laughter and the busy sound of *boeremusiek*, a rumor of melancholy strains and the sullen wavering rhythms of dancers approaching the bungalow in hesitant steps like the footsteps of a weary soldiery. Then they were at the door. The sound of boots thundered in my ears. I was

seized by the neck, yanked off the body of the girl, and
thrown right against the wall. A fist crashed into my face,
a well-aimed boot, and I subsided into a sweet state of
unconsciousness.

24

Death by hanging!

That is to be my crown of thorns. Death, at any rate, for the unpardonable crime of having been born black in a world where White Is Right and White Is Might. Better to have been born a beetle, crawling too close to the ground to notice the purity of the sky. Better by far not to have noticed that first mischievous gleam in the eye of that English girl.

Yes, I'm to die. I'll die a victim not of this white woman's lunatic lies and my own worthless passion for what remained always a light beyond my reach, a light beyond the horizon; all that can be forgiven. Love, passion, simplicity, even ignorance can be forgiven. They are not the things for which one is too ashamed to die. But they are not what I will die for. No, I'll die of a vaster, deeper, more cruel conspiracy by the rulers of my country who have made a certain knowledge between persons of different races not only impossible to achieve but positively dangerous even to *attempt* to acquire. They have made contact between the races a cause for profoundest alarm amongst white citizens.

This girl, for example, white, pretty, consumed by her own vanity and the need to escape from a life of numbing boredom, will be responsible, some will argue, for the dispatch of one more young African life to perdition. Such a view is quite mistaken. Veronica is responsible, of course, in a way, but only marginally, symbolically, responsible. The bearer of a white skin and the bearer of the flesh and blood of a gypsy, the bearer also, if I may so add, of a curse and a wound of which, not being very bright, she was not particularly aware, this English girl has simply been an instrument in whom is revealed in its most flagrant form the rot and corruption of a society that has cut itself off entirely from the rest of humanity, from any possibility for human growth. It is true, had the girl not appeared on the beach that first day, I would not be here now, awaiting death by hanging. I would not be counting the seconds, the minutes, the hours, wondering how the earth will feel beneath my feet on the day of my execution, what kind of sky will look down upon my liquidation. All the same, the girl was there only by chance. But having been there, she became a convenient pretext for the state to indulge its well-documented appetite for murder and destruction; she became useful as the most seductive bait ever placed in the path of a full-blooded African.

Let me hasten to add that there are no lessons to be learned from history, only images to be relearned and repeated. When I am gone, there will be others, young blacks who will not see too many suns before they, too, are cut down, before the noose is cast around their necks and the knot is tightened. No one will care then, as no one cares for me now, except perhaps the few relatives and friends. After the rope, there will be no fire. No stones will break. The graves will not open. Certainly my family and friends will mourn, my mother will probably faint with grief, but not much else will mark my passage from this world. It is true one person will feel compelled to commemorate this wretched drama for what it's worth. My pal, Dr. Emile Dufré, will soon be packing his copious notes and many index cards. He will carefully arrange the photographs and mementos of the girl on the beach, which I gave to him in a moment of unthinking affection. He will carry to the plane with him the numerous newspaper clippings, the photocopies of the documentary evidence and court transcripts. Upon his arrival in Zurich, he will write up his memories of the place, his careful analyses, his daring interpretations, all devoted to the reconstruction of a fractured personality, which became the subject of a most intensive investigation, all for the glorification of scientific method. Quite possibly, upon the publication of this study, Dr.

Dufré will receive from his academic peers throughout the enlightened world the accolade of one whose labors deserve the highest recognition for having conducted such an illuminating study of the benighted tormented mind of an African criminal. At least one person, I am glad to say, will benefit from this whole sorry affair.

To many people I may sound unusually buoyant, even cheerful, I know. But I am not. As the days go by and the appointed hour for my execution draws near, I feel my loneliness even more intolerably. Every Wednesday my mother comes, supported on each arm by the Cato Manor women led by the doughty Ma-Mlambo. The visits are the hardest part of a day normally devoted to reflection, to the writing of my life story, to the cordial interviews with Dufré, my constant companion, my interrogator, my father-confessor. Seeing my mother like that, her bowed head wrapped in a black *doek,* the rest of her figure swathed in a long blanket as if to shield her from the eyes of the world, makes my heart sink within me. It is as if she were the one being prepared for slaughter, not I. This woman, who sacrificed so much and gained so little from it, who bore me, raised me, toiled like a slave to send me through school, will know nothing of a peaceful old age. She will grow old with the bitter knowledge that she gave birth to a son only to see him hang, and for what exactly she will never know. For the love of a white woman? God, no, not for that! For love, I repeat, anything can be forgiven. But love is not what I felt for this girl. To such a cheap, worthless emotion only the name of lust can be given. For mere servile desire is what I will hang for, that impossible dream of all disconsolate, dissatisfied young men, which is the attainment of the forbidden fruit, a hunger and thirst enjoyed more in its contemplation than in its satisfaction.

Anyway, very soon now all this will be over. Ashes to ashes, dust to dust, the priest will intone. I am grateful for one thing. Prison, after all, is not so bad when you are to hang. Much better this isolation, this quarantine, which is like the waiting at a small railway station before the start of a long journey, than to be plucked suddenly from the bosom of the family and friends and then dispatched to the scaffold. Here I already feel on the edge of a precipice. The outside world is a shadow without reality, a patch of blue sky seen through the bars of a prison window, a slash of sunshine caught suddenly in the unnatural silence of a working day, or a swath of moonbeam penetrating into a darkened cell through the high window grill at night. The world is a rumor of trains arriving and departing, of ships honking in the black harbor, of voices, laughter, and the sudden blast of a siren from an all-night production line. But occasionally, more cheering voices can be heard from other parts of the prison: political prisoners lustily singing freedom songs. *"Izokunyathel 'iAfrika, Van Rooyen!"* (Africa will step on you, Van Rooyen.) *"Thina Sizwe!"* *"Sikhalela umhlaba wethu!"* (We the Africans mourn for the lost Africa.) *"Mabayek 'umhlaba wethu!"* (They must leave our land alone.) Voices individually weak and at first very tentative, but once united combine into a single powerful sound rolling and thundering, shaking the very foundations of the prison walls. Yes, those voices keep me company. I couldn't ask for a better send-off to the next world than those voices announcing the near-dawn of freedom, and then, of course, the unruly birds, which I see daily mating in the sky!